THE LAW TRAIL

THE LAW TRAIL

LAURAN PAINE

THORNDIKE
CHIVERS

This Large Print edition is published by Thorndike Press, Waterville, Maine USA and by BBC Audiobooks Ltd, Bath, England.
Thorndike Press is an imprint of Thomson Gale, a part of The Thomson Corporation.
Thorndike is a trademark and used herein under license.

LIBRARY OF CONGRESS CATALOGING-IN-PUBLICATION DATA

Paine, Lauran.
   The law trail / by Lauran Paine.
      p. cm. — (Thorndike press large print westerns)
   ISBN 0-7862-8985-6 (lg. print : alk. paper)
   1. Large type books. I. Title.
PS3566.A34L396 2006
813'.54—dc22   2006019219

BRITISH LIBRARY CATALOGUING-IN-PUBLICATION DATA AVAILABLE

Published in 2006 in the U.S. by arrangement with Golden West Literary Agency.
Published in 2007 in the U.K. by arrangement with Golden West Literary Agency.

U.K. Hardcover: 978 1 405 63934 7 (Chivers Large Print)
U.K. Softcover: 978 1 405 63935 4 (Camden Large Print)

Printed in the United States of America on permanent paper.
10 9 8 7 6 5 4 3 2 1

THE LAW TRAIL

ONE:
THE CRIME

No one knew how Jake Sunday had died. All they were certain of was that several hours after church, when it was possible for the saloon's patrons to sidle around and enter the building without earning a lot of righteous and blistering condemnation, which would have accrued had they gone directly to the saloon from church, it was discovered that Jake had been shot to death.

Murder, folks said, because although Jake's backbar pistol and sawed-off shotgun were still conspicuously in place on the shelf beneath the bar, neither of them had evidently been touched and for an obvious fact neither of them had been fired, yet Jake was lying on the sawdust floor behind his bar, flat out and face-up, dead of two bulletholes in the chest.

When word was carried to Walt Harney, the deputy stationed in Millton, and he hastened forward, his first concern was to herd everyone out of the saloon and close the roadway doors, then to roll a smoke while gazing at Jake, wondering why he and evidently no one else had heard any gunshots.

When a man was shot in the brisket at close range inside a building on a Sunday morning, there was every reason to believe the thunderous echoes would carry, even over the distantly muted sounds of psalmsingers up at the church.

Walt Harney found the answer to this riddle when he walked out through the hanging drape into the back-room where Jake kept his surplus casks and boxes of bottled whisky. This room had foot-thick walls filled with sawdust because in former times when Millton had been a military post, the saloon had been the comissary's warehouse and Jake's storeroom had been where sides of smoked meat had been stored, safe from excessive heat.

Walt Harney had little difficulty discerning the tracks. Jake had not been shot out front, behind his bar, he had been shot in the insulated storeroom, then dragged out and left lying behind the bar.

Why his killer had gone to this bother was to Walt Harney a minor mystery. He expected to understand the reason eventually,

but for the time being it actually was unlikely to facilitate his identification of a
killer.

He smoked and sat in the storeroom for a
long while, then went to the adjoining cub-
byhole which had been Jake's office, and sat
in there for another hour reading invoices,
receipts, and searching for personal notes
or letters, or even for a personal journal. All
he found were two neat stacks, one for
unpaid bills, the other for paid bills. Jake
Sunday had left no personal notes or letters
behind, which did not mystify Walt Harney
because Jake had told him upon several oc-
casions that he had no living relatives. Also,
Walt had known Jake for seven years and in
all that time had not heard Jake talk about
himself, his family or his past.

Walt had to abandon his quest for next-
of-kin, and eventually he also had to give
up on his quest for any kind of a clue which
would offer a hint as to why Jake had been
killed.

There was always someone willing to commit a killing. Jake Sunday had been a physi-
cally powerful, scarred brawler with twenty-
five years of experience in the saloon
business; he had enemies, inevitably. No one
liked being knocked down with a wagon-
spoke, or being punched out through the

doors. Jake had been hard on troublemakers ever since Walt Harney had known him. In fact Walt had always approved of Jake's methods because they largely eliminated the necessity for Walt constantly to be on hand, especially on Saturday night when the rangeriders congregated to let off steam after a long arduous week.

Walt went back out front, helped himself to a beer while standing beside the corpse underfoot, then took the glass around in front of the bar from habit — Jake had never allowed anyone behind his bar — and there, as he sipped beer and finished his smoke, he began to worry because out of the thousands of patrons Jake Sunday had known and served over a quarter of a century behind his bar, the chance of finding just one solitary individual who might have been carrying a murderous grudge for years, appeared to be astronomically high against Walt ever finding him.

He finished the beer and made another tour of the silent old building, even going upstairs to Jake's private quarters and doing some rummaging up there, but all he found was a horsehead rosette of the kind some men used to hold a browband to the cheekpiece of a bridle. It was oval, made of glass, and had the upraised head and flowing white mane of an elegant horse pictured inside the glass. It was not an unusual item, except that Walt found it under Jake's body, and there was only one rosette, which would be a little like having half a bridle.

He searched Jake without finding the matching rosette. He had the thing in his hand when he went upstairs looking for another rosette up there, and when he finally returned to the lower floor having had no success whatever upstairs, he put the rosette upon the bar and stood looking at it irritably, speculating that it probably had no particular significance — except that it had been beneath the dead man.

There could be a half-dozen reasonable explanations for the thing to be under Jake, but it stuck in Walt Harney's mind that there was probably a connection between the horsehead rosette and Jake Sunday's killing. How and why there should be a connection he could not imagine.

The notorious manhunter and hired killer Tom Horn had marked his slayings by placing a small green stone beneath each corpse. Perhaps someone had done the same thing with Jake Sunday, using the glass rosette. If so, he had to be rather flamboyant for a hired gunman.

Walt drew himself another glass of beer

and took it with him to the lower end of the bar where he raised the glass a little in the direction of the dead barman, drank, then walked back in the direction of the insulated storeroom.

Jake had been shot twice at close range. The punctures, particularly the ones in back, were large, indicating that Jake had been killed by either a .44 or perhaps a .45. Despite the thickness of his powerful body both slugs had exited, therefore somewhere in the storeroom, in a wall most likely, there should be two embedded slugs.

He found them, but they were not in any of the three walls he initially searched, instead they were in the wall which was opposite the doorway leading into the storeroom, and that motivated Walt to stand in thought for a while.

Earlier, he had assumed that whoever had shot Jake had been in the storeroom with him, at Jake's invitation most likely. Jake and the other person had been talking, arguing probably, when the other person had drawn and fired, twice.

But now it appeared that the killer may never have entered the storeroom. He could have remained beyond the door and when Jake walked to the door, the killer could have shot him twice without even opening his mouth to Jake or without entering the storeroom.

Walt finished the beer and took it back to the bar, left the glass there and rolled a cigarette. He was satisfied that he had resolved two difficulties; that Jake had not been killed where he was now lying, and how the killing had been accomplished.

He lit up and exhaled blue smoke. The trouble with matters of this kind was that for every minor solution there either remained, or appeared, an entire fistful of major mysteries.

Why, for example, had Jake been dragged out behind his bar; what did the horsehead-rosette mean; and above everything else, why was Jake killed?

Walt left the saloon by the back-alley doorway, knowing better than to leave by the front door. There would be people in the front roadway. Within another hour or so even using a back-alley would not prevent him from being accosted. Everyone in town knew Jake. Not everyone was fond of him, but he had a large coterie of friends, all male. The wives and mothers and sweethearts around town had little use for Jake; he had been outspokenly critical of them. Only last month when the buxom wife of the blacksmith's helper had loudly denounced Jake and his 'evil bawdy house of a saloon' for the condition her husband had been in when he'd arrived home after work one night, Jake had come right back with a remark all the married men understood, and most of the married women also understood although wild horses could not have dragged acknowledgement out of them.

'Lady,' Jake had exclaimed, 'the only time a man who works hard doesn't want to go home at the end of the day is when what he's got at home ain't even as warm and pleasant as a glass of beer!'

Walt remembered being as shocked over that statement as most other folks had been. He also remembered privately laughing over it, later, when the shock had passed, and down at the liverybarn old Ned Allen who owned the place threatened to have those words immortalized by painting them on the inside of his barn.

Jake had been a single man. Of his past no one knew much because Jake never discussed his past. He was a man's man; he was forthright, roughly funny at times, smelled of tobacco and whisky, and loved to talk horses. He did not lie, and kept his word. If Jake had been colourful it was inadvertent; he never spoke when there was anything being said worth listening to, and

14

he did nothing to make himself characteristically outstanding. In fact Jake had not liked colourful people, whom he equated with fourflushers.

By the time Walt got down the road where he could cross over to his office at the Millton jailhouse it had occured to him that a woman might have shot Jake, except when women used handguns they didn't ordinarily use anything as big and clumsy and heavy as a .44 or a .45.

There was another small mystery to trouble the deputy sheriff. Jake's backbar money-drawer had evidently not even been opened. There had been sixty-five dollars in silver, gold, and paper 'shinplasters' in the drawer.

Normally when a successful businessman was murdered robbery was the motive. Walt swore under his breath, shook his head and entered the jailhouse.

TWO:
THE ROSETTE

Ned Allen was a shuffling, slovenly individual with hard, shrewd, practical eyes, and an aged mouth which showed the precise extent to which he had been disillusioned in life.

At sixty-five Ned, like most other men who hadn't lived secluded and protected lives, had all the scars to show that the things he had encountered on his travels through the years to his present age, had seldom been more than passingly rewarding.

When he walked into Walt Harney's office with his complaint, his attitude went no deeper than disgust and bitter resentment. Ned could no longer be surprised nor deluded. He said, 'Well, some son of a bitch stole a good blood-bay off me last night some time,' and took a chair as he made this announcement as though he were more resigned to the loss than he was of the opinion that the law would ever get his horse back for him.

Walt, having expected something altogether different, having expected some comment about the passing of Jake who had been a friend of Ned's, briefly pondered the possibility of there being a connection between one crime and the other crime.

'What time?' he asked, and got a vinegary look.

'I sleep nights,' replied Ned, considering the younger man from perpetually narrowed

16

small eyes, 'I don't go prowling around. I don't know what time the horse was taken. I went out back this morning first thing, and there was the corral gate open and the blood-bay gone.' Ned shifted in the chair. 'Tracks all over the place. Thirty-five years ago when I scouted for the army I could have followed that sign all the way to hell and back. About all I can tell you now is that he was a husky feller, not any taller'n you are, and his boots was run-down . . . Oh yeah; and he saddled and bridled the blood-bay out back, then rode northwesterly, which would be the natural route, wouldn't it? Overman being out in that direction, somewhere.'

Overman was an outlaw-town. If anyone in the Millton countryside had ever visited Overman back in its secret mountain-meadow, he had never told about it, so all people actually had to go by was hearsay, and that was varied as hearsay never failed to be.

Just one thing seemed irrefutable: The outlaw-town *did* exist. It was somewhere deep in the Chiricahua Mountains, presumably not too distant from the Mexican line, although no one knew that for a fact, either.

Walt had long been of the opinion that most of the claims about Overman were false or at the very least, exaggerated. For example, no cow outfit was ever rustled clean that it was not immediately claimed that there had been the dust of a driven herd visible along the far rims where thieves were taking their beeves to the Overman area.

Every stagecoach robbery in Arizona Territory was allegedly committed by notorious fugitives residing back in the mountains at Overman. Most murders were also committed by Overman's residents, and when posses failed to overtake fleeing felons, they were invariably reported as having been headed for Overman at the last sighting.

Now, when Ned just naturally made his remark about the stolen blood-bay being ridden in the direction of the secret mountains, Walt blew out a big breath in resignation, and said, 'Ned, even if he *started* out riding northwest, between here and the mountains he could have turned off in the different directions.'

Ned said, 'Why?'

'Why? Why because he could, that's why!'

Ned squinted harder. 'You know he didn't take my horse up there, do you?'

'No damn it, and you don't know that he *did* take it up there, either,' exclaimed Walt, then curbed his temper. He waited, then said, 'Was the horse shod; what condition was he in; how far do you expect the thief could get on him, and what was wrong with the animal?'

Ned scratched a bristly jaw before trying to order his thoughts in the sequence those questions had been made, and when he failed he simply said, 'He was fresh-shod only couple days back, and he's a fairly young horse, seven or eight . . . He'd buck. I don't know where he come from nor who broke him, but somewhere down the line he had learned to pitch. He'd only do it under certain circumstances. I learned the trick of that darned horse after he bucked folks off a few times when I was tryin' to peddle him.'

'What was the trick?'

'Don't put no cold saddle-blanket on his back first thing in the morning. If you done that, he'd take to you like a demon. I always warmed the pads by the stove in the harness-room first, *then* rigged him out. By gawd he was as nice a ride as you'd ever want to set on, Walt. But only if you was careful. Thin-skinned I expect.'

Walt frowned slightly. 'How come he didn't buck off the thief if the man stole him in the night and saddled up with a cold blanket?'

Ned sighed. 'That's just it, he didn't use

no cold pad. I found an old wore-out snake turned into my haystack with fresh saddle marks. That thief rode the wore-out critter, then just switched his outfit to the blood-bay, and hell — the saddle-blanket was still warm.'

Walt said, 'Wait a minute. If he killed Jake, then he just might not get any further than one day's ride.'

Ned screwed up his face. 'What the hell are you talking about?'

'I'm talking about in the morning when he saddles up and climbs aboard to ride on —'

'I understand that,' interrupted Ned irritably. 'Damn it I'm the one who told you about it. And that's what I had in mind when I come up here this morning; to cozzen you into goin' after him and takin' your time, then in the mornin' be settin' on a rock close by watchin' when he toes into the stirrup.'

Ned shifted position and winced as he came down hard on a round object in his pocket, and said, 'What do you mean — if he killed Jake?'

'Jake's dead,' stated the deputy.

Ned replied curtly. 'I know that. Everyone in town is talkin' about it. But why this feller who stole my horse; he was a stranger. You'd ought to see that horse he had to abandon. It's rode right down to bones and numbness. My guess is that he's an outlaw on the run.'

'Why would he kill Jake?' asked Walt.

'Who said he did?' demanded the old liveryman. 'If he did, well hell, it'd be to rob Jake. I never seen that brand before, the one on his abandoned old snake. He's on the run sure as hell. *If* he killed Jake, it was to rob him, only my guess is that he was in far too much of a hurry to hunt up a saloonman to rob him. He'd been riding hard, and when he left here he was still riding hard — on my horse, the bastard.'

Ned shifted position again, cursed when he winced this time and dug in a trouser pocket, brought forth the hard little round object he had been bruising himself with, and pitched it over on the desk in front of Walt Harney.

'That there rosette was lyin' in the dirt about where that blasted thief dumped his outfit before leadin' my blood-bay over where his outfit lay, to saddle up.'

Walt sat gazing at the rosette. He had its mate in his pocket!

'You ever see that thing before?' Walt asked the liveryman. Ned had a number of sets of those things at his harness-room, not on riding-horse-bridles but on several sets of work-and driving-harness.

'No, not that particular one. I've seen lots of rosettes in my time, and mostly they aren't too different, but this here one isn't one I've seen before.'

'It didn't fall off some harness of yours, then?'

'I just told you, Walt, I never seen that rosette before.'

Walt picked up the rosette, brought forth the mate to it from his pocket, compared them under the widening stare of Ned Allen, then pocketed them both and turned to reach for his hat.

'Where did you get that other one?' the liveryman asked, arising with a little effort from his chair.

Instead of replying Walt held the door and after Ned had passed through on to the yonder plankwalk, Walt said, 'Show me the corral where he stole the blood-bay, and his tracks.'

As they walked southward with the town Sunday-silent on all sides of them, a number of disoriented townsmen milled elsewhere, lost because the saloon was locked and dark.

Millton also had a card-room and a pool-hall, but neither of those establishments was open this Sunday. There evidently was something infinitely evil about cards and pool on Sundays which was not clearly visible to the average person, because by town ordinance no gambling house could operate on the Sabbath, but the saloon was allowed to be open all day long on any Sunday Jake had chosen to keep it open.

Protesting women of the Ladies Altar Society were once told by Abe Dunphy who owned the emporium and was also head of the Town Council that the Lord himself had condoned liquor; he was always mentioning it in the Bible as wine, so the saloon could remain open on Sunday, but the preacher Abe had talked with had been vehement in his statements concerning the Lord's loathing of gamblers.

Now, the discreet locals who had put together little poker and twenty-one games in the corners of Jake's place, every Sunday, were lost and adrift.

Ned had been one of them. This morning, on his walk southward beside the deputy sheriff, when he was unable to elicit anything from Walt concerning that pair of horsehead rosettes, he looked across the road, saw the idling men in their go-to-meeting attire, and made a clucking sound.

'We're sure going to miss Jake,' he mournfully said. 'No more Sunday fan-tan and twenty-one.'

'It was against town ordinances anyway,' stated Walt, and old Ned shrugged stooped shoulders. Ned was a law-abiding man like everyone else in town and out upon the range, which meant he obeyed every law and each ordinance which it suited him to obey, or which did not invade what Ned considered his harmless right to do something he darned well felt like doing and which clearly did not harm another living individual.

'I'll tell you what's a lot more illegal — stealing my blood-bay horse,' he growled as they turned in across the shady big old horse-trading yard, bound down through the barn and out back.

Ned led for the last hundred yards. Where he stopped rigidly pointing, the ground showed evidence of saddle-skirts having squatted in the dust, and worn boots milling here and there. Ned pointed to a particularly clear horeshoe imprint. 'Still see the knurled marks on the nailheads,' he said, leaning far down and squinting. 'Well, if I had some glasses I'd be able to see them. Those shoes was just put on.'

Walt leaned, saw how correct Ned was without being able to see the marks himself, then he turned and studied the imprints where the man had dumped his saddle. Ned scouted around and back like an old dog seeking a scent. 'There,' he suddenly exclaimed with a sound of ringing triumph in his voice. 'Right there; you see that smooth place in the dust? That's right where that rosette was lying.' Ned pointed with a gnarled finger.

Walt walked back to look at the abandoned horse, shook his head that anyone would use a horse like that, then walked over where Ned had traced out the tracks as far as the northward alleyway.

Ned straightened back and lifted an accusing finger to point towards the soft-hazed distant mountains. 'Straight as an arrer,' he announced. 'Exactly like I told you he went. Right towards those hills and through them to the mountains and right through them to —'

'To Overman,' groaned Walt.

The older man turned quickly. 'You finally seen the light, have you?'

Walt considered that blue-blurry distance as he said, 'No. I just said what you were going to tell me, Ned.' He looked around. 'How about having your dayman saddle my bay?'

Ned bobbed his head. 'Take a rifle, Walt, don't rely on one of them lousy little runt-barrelled saddleguns. Take a rifle and you can reach him from half a mile.'

Walt sighed. 'The bay horse, Ned. I'll be back for him in a few minutes.'

He walked northward up the alley to the rear of his jailhouse building, let himself in from out back with a large old brass key, selected the booted carbine from the rack, took the belly-gun-derringer from a desk-drawer, slung his light blanketroll under one arm and the last thing he took off the wall was his worn and faded and stained old blanketcoat. This was springtime, which meant the Arizona days were beautiful, but the nights after midnight were cold by any standards and would remain that way for another couple of months.

He returned to the barn, ignored the garrulousness of the liveryman, who was now also accompanied by his dayman, another older man, but thinner and, thankfully, far less talkative, swung up and rode his horse out into the rear alley. Behind him Ned and the dayman leaned to watch.

He rode up as far as the little cottage beside the church, rattled the back door from the saddle and when the curly-headed, powerfully-built minister appeared still in his grey preaching suit and his backward celluloid collar, Walt said, 'Bruce, I got to be out of town until maybe tomorrow night. Someone stole a horse off Ned. I was wondering if you'd look after Jake; see that he gets a decent burial and all if I don't happen to return until maybe the middle of next week.'

The powerfully-built minister nodded. 'I'll take care of it,' he said. 'Which is most important, Walt, a horse-thief or a murderer?'

Walt smiled drily. 'Both, I'd say, if there's much of a chance for them to be the same feller.'

The minister looked rueful. 'Sorry. Don't worry, I'll see that Jake is properly cared for . . . Be careful, Walt.'

Harney lifted his rein-hand. 'I've been saying that to myself for the past hour, Bruce,' he replied, grinned and squeezed both knees against the horse to ride on up out of town to the open country beyond where the Sunday-silence wasn't confined just to Sundays, and where visibility was excellent for many miles.

The only thing he hadn't brought along was food. The reason he hadn't done that was because he knew every cow outfit in each direction he might have to ride for a hundred miles, and he also knew which ones fed the best when a hungry lawman rode into the yard.

THREE:
SHADE AND SHADOWS

Walt Harney was no tracker. Not in the sense that Ned had once been, but there had been very little real need for skilled trackers since the entire Southwest had become fairly well settled and populated. Telegraphers hunched over brass keys had been doing the work of trackers for a quarter of a century now, and in the places where there was no telegraph to rouse a countryside, there were cow outfits whose riders almost invariably volunteered to be possemen on a manhunt, in order to break the monotony of rangeriding.

In this case, however, there was neither the telegrapher at Millton to send word far ahead that an outlaw was fleeing on a stolen blood-bay gelding, and in the direction Walt Harney initially rode, there were no cow outfits either, at least there were no head-quarters of cow outfits, although otherwise every yard of the vast open country either belonged to a cow outfit, or was being held in lease or in some other way by the cow outfits.

The only unclaimed open land still extant was in the mountains, and it was usually poor cattle-country, with water in the wrong places, with predators by the score, and in summertime also with the deadly chance of sweeping big destructive fires.

There was another deterrent. Hold-outs were still back in the mountains. Not very many of them, according to all the authorities, army and civilian alike, but there never had to be very many suicidal Apache hold-outs. In fact there only had to be one, with a gun in his hands and a burning, white-hot fury in his heart, to eliminate riders into the mountains, past the lowland foothills.

Among the legends surrounding the outlaw town of Overman, was the one about the renegades in their village paying hold-outs to provide a deadly buffer between Overman and the southward grasslands.

Walt had always been very sceptical of that story, but he had never doubted but that there were secret rancherias back in the mountains where hold-outs existed in stealth like wild animals. He had seen a few hold-outs, himself, over the past six or seven years when he'd had to ride into the mountains. He had never been fired on, and he had never tried to sneak up on one of them.

As the plain trail he was now following began to eventually swerve back around from the northeast to the northwest, he had two thoughts: he was very glad Ned wasn't along to start cackling about 'I told you so', and the other thought had to do with snake-eyed Apaches lying in the rocks, or in tree-shade up ahead, or perhaps simply sitting fully exposed upon a rock in warm sunshine, watching the lone horseman heading towards the mountains.

Anyone crossing up out of Millton towards the hills who did not stay on the stageroad or who did not veer off before reaching the foothills, was bound to be of interest to anyone up there who had nothing better to do than sit and watch, for the very simple reason that the land from the foothills southward was as open and free of trees or undergrowth as most seas of range-country grass usually were.

Those hold-outs were not fools. While they frequently aroused loud howls and lamentations over the line down in Mexico where they raided and plundered and fought the authorities, they had never been proven to be either horse-thieves or cattle-thieves in the area where they had their secret camps. If they had raided in the Millton

30

country, for example, they would have hired gunmen and other Indians, also working for cattle-interests, hunting them relentlessly.

Walt recalled some of the tales he'd heard as he steadily rode through morning warmth and brilliance. From experience he knew very well that most of the scoffers who had been swearing for years there were no Apaches back in those mountains, had been under constant Apache surveillance every time they rode along the foothills, without having any inkling of it.

He had that feeling, himself, about noon, when he was finally close enough to make out landmarks in the lower broken country. He would have bet the price of a new saddle he was under surveillance. It did not especially bother him. The hold-outs were not warlike; once, they had been and the results had been stunningly devastating. Now, they hunted and hid and moved constantly and avoided every contact.

He did not feel especially sorry for them, but neither had he relayed the information cowmen and travellers had brought to him to the army, each time someone saw an Apache.

He was much more concerned with the route of the horse-thief. If he had been an excellent tracker he probably would have been able to make faster progress. As it was, he lost the sign more often then he rode it, and even when he dismounted and led the horse as he concentrated very hard on *not* losing it, the tracks disappeared every time he encountered tall grass or hardpan.

He would usually find it again before too long, perhaps because the horse-thief had not worried about leaving a trail. As a rule horse-thieves scarcely worried about being *tracked* down, they worried about being *run* down. As long as a pursuer was tracking, he was behind, but when he guessed ahead and made a chase out of it, he quite often got within rifle-range, and *that* mattered.

Walt Harney, however, had another reason for not fretfully pushing hard in pursuit. He simply wanted to be close enough by nightfall so that in the morning if he could climb a tree, perhaps, or get upon a sidehill with a sweeping view, he would be able to catch the sight of violent movement when the horse-thief saddled up.

It was early afternoon when he came to the little sump-spring called Mexican Well. Here, he saw the fairly fresh imprints of those new shoes, and as Ned had pointed out back in town, it was still possible to detect the knurled criss-crosses atop each horseshoe-nailhead.

He made a smoke here, for his mid-day meal, allowed his horse to drag the reins and crop grass after drinking, and Walt stepped up beside a mighty-old man-high rock to stand silently and comfortably blocking in specific areas of the onward countryside, waiting to detect movement.

He did not find any movement, except for a small band of pronghorn antelope who were raising a thin dust eastward as they fled along the base of the nearest foothills at twice the speed of the fastest horse.

The tracks left the sump-spring bearing westerly again. There was a possibility that they would also veer eastward when they got up there, but Walt had his doubts.

He was beginning to think as a horse-thief might do, and if the horse-thief knew about the secret town of Overman, this would be exactly the way he would ride to get there after leaving Millton.

Walt went back to the horse, snugged up, led the animal a short distance and swung up across the hot saddle-leather to ride in the approximate direction he was certain the horse-thief had ridden.

He made only an occasional cursory attempt to detect the sign he was supposed to be following, and when he finally got to the broken country where there was tree-shade, for a change, and underbrush, he wondered if that feeling between the shoulder-blades was prompted by hold-outs spying on his progress, or — more to be feared, he thought — it was occasioned by the horse-thief up ahead somewhere, shrewdly guessing about where Walt would pass below the biggest rock so the outlaw could shoot him out of the saddle as he went by.

It did not happen, perhaps because Walt refused to go anywhere near the obvious bushwhacking-sites. From here on he did not have to qualify as a tracker, all he had to be good at was heeding his instinctive fears.

The last time he saw the sign of those new horse-shoes, the blood-bay had been tethered beside an old bull-pine, out of sight, while the man in the worn-out boots had turned back downslope a hundred or so yards, had hunkered in the shade gazing out over the open grassland below, and had smoked a cigarette whose brown-paper stub he had left plunged into the ancient dust.

Without any doubt the horse-thief had been watching Walt's progress, but that did not intrigue Walt as much as the fact that, with at the very least a six-hour head-start, the outlaw had got no further. By Walt's most conservative estimate the horse-thief should have been so far ahead by now he would have been lost in the huge, bulky distances.

Walt also had a smoke where the horse-thief had squatted, and also like his prey, he studied the rangeland, except that Walt had no solitary, persistent rider to watch. There was nothing out there, even those prong-horns were no longer anywhere in sight. They, or their dust.

Walt returned to his comfortably drows-ing horse, swung up and poked along through the warm and fragrant banks of pines and firs and hardwoods, able to make out disturbed places in the ancient patch-work of needles and leaves where a rider had passed through.

Then, when he was certain he would now be able eventually to get close enough by nightfall, the horse-thief struck a ledge of very loose tallus; every step made by man or animal across this area over the past ten centuries had been obliterated the moment a foot or a hoof was withdrawn to allow the dusty, dry stone instantly to fill in and smooth out.

He stopped upon the far side of the tallus-field and made a long, shrewd study of the skyline, of the onward terrain, and began to suspect that perhaps the horse-thief knew no more about finding the outlaw town back in here than Walt knew.

The only consistent thing the outlaw had done so far was ride in an approximately general direction — northwesterly — which would have been the same direction Walt would have chosen if he had been seeking Overman.

But these were immense mountains. Not just many miles deep and across, but hundreds of miles in other directions as well. If the fugitives who were safe in their hidden town did not care to be discovered, it would not be very difficult for them to make certain no one found the correct trail.

But Walt Harney was really much less worried about the legendary outlaw-town than he was in not being able to catch sight of his prey. By his calculations if he could sight the horse-thief, and probable murderer, before sunup in the morning, neither he nor the outlaw would ever get much closer to the outlaw-town than they would be by this evening, and that being so, Walt would have his prisoner and be heading back for Millton by mid-morning, tomorrow.

He rode eastward for several miles, not because there were any tracks to entice him, but because there were nothing but serrated cliff-faces the way he had been riding.

When he crested a low ride and started down the far side he entered a beautiful little meadow with white-oaks and tall grass growing where a narrow little white-water creek bisected the grassland.

Here, only the Lord knew how long ago, there had been a rancheria; he found the old sunken places where Apache dome-shaped brush-shelters had stood.

He prowled the soft creek-bank on both sides for fresh shod-horse marks and found nothing but animal tracks. Since the horse-thief had to have also crossed up through here, he evidently had not stopped to water his horse or to let it graze. As he went back to his own animal he decided the blood-bay was going to be treated about as cruelly and indifferently as that abandoned horse back at Millton had been treated, and that annoyed him too; he was a lifelong horseman and considered the worst crime a person could commit was cruelty to dependent animals.

FOUR:
SOMETHING UNEXPECTED

Shadows lengthened after Walt rode away

from the delightful little meadow. He rode facing the miles-distant massive upthrust of the farthest heights, and they dwarfed him down to less than ant-size and inspired in him a unique sense of unimportance.

If he never recovered the blood-bay, never caught up with the outlaw who had probably murdered Jake Sunday, nothing very much in the world would be changed. He shook off this mountain-inspired fatalism, recognizing it for what it was, having felt it before in places like this.

The sun sank steadily towards a slot in the western hilltops but long before it departed shadows came as stealthily as smoke to pool and spread among the lower canyons and even down where there were deep vales and valleys.

By the time Walt had decided which skyline landmark would be his pilot-stone his horse was beginning to evince interest in stopping for the night. Later, when they came through immense stones larger and taller than a man on a horse and walked into a grassy clearing, Walt decided they would halt. Without much doubt they could have covered another three or four miles, but there was always the possibility that they would not find another meadow to stop in before nightfall forced them to halt.

Here, when he had hobbled the horse and was pulling grass-swatches to cleanse its back of salt-sweat, the horse dropped its head and greedily ate. There was a creek close by, Walt could hear it tumbling over stones and surmised it was probably a continuation of the creek he had encountered earlier, but he made no move to hunt it up until he had finished caring for the horse, had unrolled his blanketroll, and had decided that he should have at least brought along a few flat tins of sardines. By then it was steely-grey in their clearing with ranks of descending dark shadows coming down from the higher slopes on all sides.

He went over to the creek and found a fairly fresh balled-up soiled piece of bloody cloth which he touched with his boot-toe but otherwise did not examine after determining what it was — a bandage of some kind.

He had up until now not even considered the likelihood that the outlaw he was hunting was injured, and the longer he stood there motionless and thoughtful in the gathering gloom, the more he doubted that in fact the outlaw *was* wounded.

There had been no earlier indications and he had found several places where the horse-thief had rested, had smoked and squatted and killed time. Also, from the appearance of that bandage, the wound it had protected had not been a slight one.

He moved away from the creek, jerked loose the tie-down holding his Colt in its holster, stepped across the creek finally and walked soundlessly out through the grass to the first stand of softwood-trees, cottonwoods and willows, which offered a shield while he stood and waited, looking in all directions and listening.

A horse strolled from some distant trees to the east without lifting its head from the grass. It evidently had not detected the scent yet of either Walt or his mount. It was too dark to make out many details of the horse except that it was riderless, so Walt began a stealthy diagonal approach until he was close enough, then he saw the dangling single plaited rein. It was an Indian horse, and since it was not stripped to graze there was an Indian close by. If it was this Indian who had left that bloody bandage at the creek, Walt guessed that he was ill in the grass somewhere, otherwise, if he had *not* left that bandage then the Indian was probably stalking Walt.

The chances were excellent though, that if the Indian were able, he had long ago seen Walt. Since he had not offered to fight, it was at least possible that he was not belligerent. If he were *not* able . . .

Walt did not know a word of Apache, but every Apache knew some English and most of them used Mexican-Spanish as their second language. Walt was about to call forth in Spanish when the Indian horse abruptly picked up the scent of another horse and nickered, then turned to hurry over to the creek, leap it, and go rushing forward to seek Walt's horse. He passed close enough for Walt to see matted hair down his left side. It wasn't matted with pitch from the trees and it wasn't matted from sweat.

Walt turned and started zig-zagging through the grass. There was danger, of course, but less he told himself from a badly injured hold-out than from a perfectly healthy one.

He found the man sitting propped against a tree. He was perfectly conscious. He was small, as most Apaches were, and he was very dark with lank black hair and snake-like muddy dark eyes. He watched Walt walk up and made no move nor sound to help Walt locate him. When Walt stopped, right hand lightly lying on his Colt, he and the Indian steadily considered one another.

There was a bad bloody wound in the

Apache's left side. He was trying to hold grass to the ragged flesh to hold back the sticky trickle of dark blood. As far as Walt could determine the Indian was unarmed. He did not look very old, perhaps in his early twenties.

Walt said, 'What happened?' and pointed to the injury. 'Shot?'

The Apache said nothing. He continued to lean and steadily stare.

Walt sighed, sank to one knee and saw the carbine in the grass on the Indian's opposite side. Without a word he leaned and lifted the Winchester, put it farther from the Apache and tried again, this time in Spanish. 'How did you get hurt?'

The Indian finally said, 'The horse; he has only been ridden two times. He threw me into a jagged mound of stones. And now I will die.'

Walt leaned closer, pushed gently at the clenched fist with the bloody grass in it, and examined the wound. He probed a little, found no broken ribs, and straightened back to wipe his hand in the grass. 'You won't die. You won't go hunting for a long while, but you won't die.'

The intent black eyes never departed from Walt's face. 'How do you know this?' the Indian asked in Spanish.

Walt had no flat answer to give so all he said was, 'Lie back. Clear back, not against the tree, and grit your teeth. I'll get some water from the creek and be right back.' As he stood up the Indian looked up at him. Walt smiled slightly. 'You'll make it. What is your name?'

'Ben.'

They regarded each other for another moment, then Walt turned and went to the creek to soak his neckerchief and bring it back dripping cold water. The Indian was lying flat out with his eyes closed and his long, thin-lipped mouth contorted in an ugly grip of teeth and muscles.

Walt washed the wound clean, wished mightily he had found the injured man while there had still been some daylight, removed his own shirt which he had put on clean that same morning, and tore it into strips. What was left of the Apache's shirt after having already been torn to make that bandage Walt had found at the creek, was filthy.

When he had to raise the man to make the binding tight the Apache opened his eyes, looked steadily at Walt, at his exposed, powerful upper body, then closed his eyes and lay back shallowly breathing because the bandage was too tight for any other kind of breathing.

Walt wiped his hands in the grass, made a cigarette and lit it, then twisted his neckerchief almost dry and wiped perspiration from his own face and neck. When the Indian opened his eyes again Walt shook his head, grinned and said in Spanish, 'Much damned hard work. The next time, you either learn to ride a greenbroke colt, or walk. You comprehend me?'

The Apache waited a long while before speaking. Then he made a weak small smile as he said, 'You ain't got a shirt now,' in English.

Walt used English too. 'You want a smoke?'

'No, don't smoke. I want whisky.'

'Sure,' assented Walt drily, 'So do I. Do you have any?'

'No.'

'Well then, bronco, neither one of us is going to make out too well, are we?'

The Apache sighed, raised a hand gingerly to explore his bandaged side, let the hand drop back and said, 'You don't belong in here.'

Walt shrugged that off. 'Who does, friend? You? All right; and from what I've seen of it so far, you're damned well welcome to it.'

'Do you know the other one?' asked the Indian.

Walt inhaled, exhaled, studied the man's very dark, coarse features, and shook his head. 'Nope; when did the other one pass through — how long ago?'

'This afternoon when I was lying at the creek. I needed help but he was riding with a carbine in his hand looking back. I let him go past.'

'Just as well,' stated Walt. 'He stole a horse and I think he also killed a man back down in Millton. Do you know where Millton is?'

'*Si*, yes . . . And you are hunting that other man?'

'Yeah.' Walt punched out his cigarette. 'You got any food, bronco?'

The Indian gestured back towards the trees and Walt arose to go looking. He found the pack lying against a huge grey boulder. He also found blood in the grass over there which indicated that the Indian had originally used this place for resting. How he had managed to get his pack off the horse was explained by a broken girth. Evidently the injured man had been unable to hold the pack any longer and when it fell he went off the horse with it.

Walt carried the pack back and opened it in front of its owner. There was *piki*-bread in a separate roll from some oily jerky. There was a small tin of pure salt. Otherwise all the pack held was spare reloaded ammunition in a neckerchief, the two ancient smelly blankets the pack was made up out of, and a letter written in English which had evidently been folded and unfolded many times. It seemed to be something important to the Apache but Walt did not look at it.

He decided to make them a small fire, over here where it would be relatively safe to build one but the moment the injured man figured out what he was preparing to do he said, 'That other one will come back in the night. He didn't go much farther ahead.' The Indian rolled his muddy dark eyes. 'Maybe a half mile, to the next clearing.' At the sceptical look he got for saying this, the Indian rolled his eyes again, trying to see northwestward. 'There is a good trail. The one you will take when you leave here. But up ahead a mile where it strings out along the sidehill working around upwards towards the next plateau — he never came out into sight up there, and I watched for him to do that. He didn't come out. That means he's at the next meadow up ahead. You light a fire and from there he can see —'

'Save your breath,' stated Walt, with

resignation, and handed the Indian some jerky. 'Chew on that until I get back.'

When he left the wounded man he was shirtless. When he returned a little later he was still shirtless, and would have to remain that way because he did not carry a spare shirt, but he had his riding jacket and he was now wearing that when he squatted and grinned.

'How do you feel?'

The Indian answered matter-of-factly, 'I need whisky.'

Walt chewed jerky. It hadn't been cured with enough pepper so it lacked the customary tangy taste of jerky. He ate none of the *piki*. He had seen the Navajos make the stuff and was sure Apaches did it pretty much the same way. For this reason he ate nothing but jerky and afterwards, perhaps as much because his injury and fever demanded it as because of the jerky, the Indian required water and Walt had to make two trips to the creek and back. Finally, though, the Indian swore about the feeling which was returning to his bruised body, which Walt decided was a good sign. When there had been nothing but numbness and lassitude he was ready to believe the Indian had lost too much blood and would die. When the Indian swore about the pain and became disagreeable about other things Walt decided he was probably going to make it.

He said, 'I can't stay with you much longer, but if you'll tell me where your rancheria is I'll take you over there. I don't think you'll be able to make it by yourself for several days, and you'll need help.'

'Don't need no help,' growled the Apache. 'You drag me to the creek where I can drink water. Leave my pack with me over there. I'll be able to go home when my strength comes back.'

Walt did that, he carried the man to the tall grass beside the creek, banked his personal things around him, pitched his blankets over him somewhat carelessly, and left. He had no admonition he felt like giving, and in his present mood the Indian was in no state of mind to accept advice or warnings.

Walt returned to his own camp upon the opposite side of the creek, made a smoke to destroy the residual taste of that badly-made jerky, and sat on the ground hunched with a blanket round his shoulders, already pushing the interlude of the Apache out of his mind and thinking instead of the man in camp somewhere up ahead of him.

It would have helped a lot if Walt had been familiar with the terrain up ahead, but he wasn't and that was that. He would have to be extremely careful, which he was prepared to be anyway because he had all night to creep up there less than a mile onward, locate his prey and if he decided after scouting the man up, not to wait for the horse with the sensitive back to do his work for him, come morning, he could do it for himself tonight.

He arose, left his carbine with his saddle and other effects in the grass, made a pass outward to make certain the horse was all right, then he turned silently to strike out across the little meadow on a northward course.

There was not a sound anywhere around, and no sign of movement. In fact, if he hadn't known he was not alone up here he would have sworn there was not another human being within miles of him.

FIVE:
A TALK BY MOONLIGHT

There was no wind to carry scents but something must have done it because in this area where nocturnal predators were very common there was not a wolf to bark his warning of an alien presence nor a coyote to do the same in his mocking manner.

Walt guessed they had detected the Indian earlier in the day, had probably detected the scent of fresh blood and had abandoned the entire area.

He did not object, the last thing he cared much about tonight was to encounter a pack of foraging wolves or some noisy little coyotes.

Without a moon to guide him, with nothing but starshine and instinct, he came across that trail leading from his lower meadow exactly where the Indian had indicated it would be, and he wasted a little time circling for sign of a shod-horse but in the darkness, while perhaps that Apache back there would have been successful, Walt was not, so he pushed onward up the trail skylining every foot of the way, less for the shielded brightness of a cooking-fire than for the bulky silhouette of a blood-bay horse.

What he eventually came across was a stone ruin where someone with a vast amount of time had laboriously erected a stone hut without using mortar. Whoever he had been, and whatever his purpose in making a hut up in here, all that remained were the four standing walls, and even they had been broken here and there.

Walt's initial thought was that the fugitive might be inside the stone *jacal,* but after scouting forward with infinite care he discovered that the only resident of that old stone ruin was a family of woodrats whose unkempt stick residence nearly filled the entire little stone hutment.

But he made one discovery. Where the same little creek which bisected the meadow back where he had left his horse skirted out and around the stone ruin, there was the very clear imprint of a rider having passed along at this place, probably to water his horse because he had immediately turned back.

Walt, who had never been much of a pedestrian, considered as much of the onward territory as he could make out before walking away from the creek and the stone ruin.

More light would have helped but since he was not going to rush ahead, limited visibility simply meant he would be unable to see farther off than he intended to go. As he worked carefully onward upon the far side of the descending trail taking care not to be positioned so that he could be skylined back there, he watched for a fire, for movement, or for a silhouette which would not particularly be endemic to this site.

All he found, eventually, was an owl skimming soundlessly low as he made his nocturnal hunt for something worth eating, and when the owl saw the man, he beat air with desperate urgency in order to achieve sufficient height to get speedily away from this place.

What eventually inclined Walt Harney to believe the Indian's deduction had been correct was not a sight, but a sound. He heard a man curse in a drawn-out low tired voice as he eased his body atop an unfurled bedroll. Walt could have been sceptical of a lot of indications that the outlaw was close by, but not this one. The only creature who swore in English was Man.

He knew approximately where that profanity had come from, took a very long while to circle around over in that direction, and eventually to sink to one knee in the grass seeking to skyline his man. But the outlaw was on the ground, he could not be projected against the paler night.

Walt inched ahead. He had to know in which direction the fugitive was facing.

He was not now thinking in terms of the bucking blood-bay horse. He was thinking in terms of an imminent capture. As long as the outlaw was in his blankets, was probably tired to the bone and either sleeping or near to it, Walt was confident enough to continue creeping onward. He had no idea there could be much difficulty even though he was clearly conscious of the fact that the outlaw had been worried about pursuit when the Indian had seen him earlier.

It was still an enigma why the fugitive was not many more miles onward, but at this particular point Walt was not at all intersted in that.

He finally saw the mounded litter of a hasty camp; the up-ended saddle, the bridle and pad, along with a pair of elegantly hand-carved saddlebags. He could also finally hear the horse greedily cropping grass in the middle distance but he could not see clearly out that far nor was he try-ing to once he knew the outlaw was very close.

There was a lingering, weak scent of tobacco smoke, as though the outlaw had smoked just before rolling in, which was commonplace.

Then a muffled cough, a clearing of a man's pipe in the growing chill of night, and it had not come from where Walt had thought the bedroll would be at all, it had come from the north, and more westerly, roughly in the same direction as the horse-sounds.

Walt settled low and waited, looking and listening. Either there were two of them, or the fugitive was not near his saddle-camp at all.

It dawned: the outlaw had made a dummy-camp. He knew there was someone pressing relentlessly over his back-trail and because he could hardly keep on riding through a black night in an unfamiliar mountainous countryside, had in fact been forced by circumstances to halt where he now was, he had reacted very sensible by setting a trap.

Walt shifted position and made his very slow and soundless way over in the new direction, and this time he was more fortunate.

He saw the blood-bay, saw the mound of indistinct proportions in the nearby grass, and when the moon indifferently soared at last, Walt also saw the pale glow of moonlight off grey steel where a carbine lay in the grass beside the indistinct lump.

Walt was wary of going closer. He had no way of knowing whether the blood-bay would accept this new presence or not. He might, after all he was accustomed to strangers down at the liverybarn. On the other hand, with just one life to gamble with, Walt decided not to gamble at all.

He got flat down, pushed his gunhand ahead and inched his way for a couple more yards, until he had that huddled lump well in sight, then he stopped, breathed deeply for a while before saying in a very soft tone of voice: 'Mister don't you move!'

The lump did not seem to possess any life. It remained absolutely still. By moonlight it was easier to discern that the composition of that lump was a man hunched inside a thick blanket, with a rider's jacket around the upper part of his covered torso.

He undoubtedly had his sixgun under the coverings. Walt allowed sufficient time to pass before giving another order. 'Bring the gun out right easy and toss it away. Remember, Mister — very easy.'

For a while the lump did not move, did not even seem capable of breathing. Then a quiet, drawling voice said, 'All right,' and movement showed that a hand and arm — and a gun — were coming forth.

Walt moved to one side. The fugitive would be foolish to try it, but to some men desperate foolishness was better than captivity.

But the gun appeared, dangled momentarily, then fell away in the grass.

'Sit up — slow,' said Walt, and to emphasize his temperament he cocked the Colt. It was a slight sound but it carried to the lump in the grass, and it was an unmistakable sound to anyone who had ever before heard a handgun cocked.

The fugitive arose out of his lumpy bed, raised a hand slowly to scratch as he explored the grass until he had his hat, and dumped that atop his awry thick head of hair.

'Who the hell are you?' the fugitive asked, with no special sound of anxiety or fear in the words. 'Are you from the village up yonder, or are you that feller who come across from the direction of Millton?'

'I'm the feller who is going to take you back to Millton,' explained Walt, and couldn't resist asking the question which had been uppermost in his thoughts for most of the afternoon. 'Why aren't you farther along? By now you should be against the rims, miles northward.'

The outlaw turned, peering in the direction of a pale indistinct face and a clearly visible cocked Colt. 'The gawddamned horse,' he exclaimed with savage bitterness. 'I rested this morning as soon as I got over into the foothills; give the lousy horse some consideration, too. I off-rigged him, used the hobbles, and lay down with the saddle-blanket over me to sleep for a couple of hours before heading northward again. The damned blood-bay wasn't tired but I was. I'd been on the trail a long while.'

Walt could surmise the rest of it, but he allowed his prisoner to finish his embittered tale.

'I got up about sunup, caught the lousy horse, saddled up, jumped astride — and holy mackerel . . . !'

'He bucked like a demon,' said Walt.

'Yeah,' confirmed the fugitive. 'Do you know him?'

'That well,' stated Walt, not quite smiling but close to it. 'Pull on your boots . . . What's your name?'

'Tom Dickson . . . Did you ever see anyone ride that lousy horse when he was taking to them?'

Walt hadn't. In fact until this very early morning he had not even known the blood-bay existed. 'Nope, but the man you stole him from told me about that trick of his. You can't saddle him up using a cold blanket; he'll bust wide open every time.'

In a conversational tone of voice as though they were old friends in camp, the fugitive said, 'Mister, I'll tell you for a fact — if I hadn't been able to grab the apple and the hand-hold behind the cantle he'd have lost me off sure as hell. Even so, he liked to have

57

wrecked me. When I rode him down and could tumble off, my back was out of fix for hours. The best I could manage was to lie there holding the darned reins . . . Now you know why I didn't get any farther along.'

Walt said, 'Yeah. Too bad.'

Dickson looked from beneath his floppy hat brim. 'Too bad for a fact. And who are you?'

'Deputy sheriff from Millton.'

Dickson sighed. 'You sure are a stubborn man, Deputy. You went to all this bother over one darned horse — who isn't worth the price of a case of beans anyway.'

Walt did not respond for a while. He watched Dickson tug at his boots, watched the fugitive look longingly and stealthily out where his Colt was lying, and when Dickson turned, facing forward Walt tossed him something. 'Catch,' he called. The outlaw obeyed from instinct. Walt waited. After Tom Dickson had leaned to look closely at the cold little smooth round object in his hand, he slowly raised his head.

'You lost both of them,' Walt explained. 'I've got the other one too.'

'Is that so?'

'Yeah, that is so. And now you know why I didn't let up once I got on your trail. It wasn't just the blood-bay; in fact it wasn't really the blood-bay at all . . . Now stand up, we're going to get saddled and turn back down out of here.'

Dickson arose, and screwed up his face. 'Go back down out of here in the damned dark?'

'Yeah.'

Walt arose, told his prisoner to haul his blankets and jacket back over where the saddle-camp was, and while Tom Dickson was doing that, Walt used his belt to make a lead-shank, and led the blood-bay over too.

Six:
Trouble on Top of Trouble

Walt instructed his prisoner to leave everything at his saddle-camp but his saddlebags and horse-outfit, and when Tom Dickson protested Walt pointed on down the trail. 'Walk. Lead the horse and walk on down to the next meadow . . . As for your bedroll and all. One way or another, you're not going to need them again.'

That seemed to be an enigmatic thing for a man to say, so Dickson scowlingly said, 'What are you talking about?'

'I'm talking about you either going to prison, or getting lynched in Millton. Either way you aren't going to need the blanketroll again, so keep walking and don't let me think you're dragging your heels.'

Tom Dickson walked, leading the blood-bay which had been re-saddled with a lukewarm saddleblanket, or maybe it hadn't bogged its head and turned inside out because no one had straddled the saddle after the saddling. In either event the blood-bay walked meekly along behind the outlaw.

Dickson did not appear to be malevolent or vicious. In fact he looked to Walt Harney like any one of dozens of rangeriders Walt had encountered down the years. When they were well along on the southward trail Walt said, 'When you reached Millton you abandoned a used up horse.'

'What of it?' asked the outlaw. 'Do you ride horses you know're ready to stumble and fall with you?'

'Where had you come from?' asked Walt, ignoring the outlaw's question.

'Where did I come from?' mused the fugitive, and paused to organize an answer.

Walt said, 'Dickson, you start playing games with me and I'll break both your arms, for openers.'

The outlaw strolled along unimpressed. 'Tall talk. You got a gun and all I got is my wits . . . Where did I come from? Deputy, I come north from Tularosa, and the reason I come hard and fast was because I had a little trouble with a Mex-feller over his wife. I figured someone from down there was after me.'

Walt scoffed. 'You figured. You either knew someone was after you or you knew they weren't after you. Which was it?'

'What's the difference? Unless there's some son of a bitch down in Millton looking for me. Then it'll be up to you.'

Walt agreed drily. 'Yep. It'll be up to me . . . To get the hell out of the way and avoid being struck by flying bullets.'

'No, damn it,' exclaimed the outlaw. 'It'll be up to you to get me safely locked up and to keep that son of a bitch away from me.'

'So he was chasing you,' mused Walt.

Dickson shrugged and jerked the blood-bay when it stumbled on the downhill trail. He was a willing conversationalist right up to this point. From here on he walked briskly down the trail and ignored the man behind him. Even when Walt asked for more details of the man pursuing him, Dickson had nothing to say.

When they reached Walt's camp Dickson stood and watched as the deputy sheriff rolled his blankets and rigged out his horse. Finally, having arrived at some kind of conclusion about Walt, he said, 'How much would it take to get you to ride back to Millton without me?'

Walt turned his horse, cast a final glance around to be sure he had not overlooked something, then said, 'A hell of a lot more than you've got. Now get on your horse.'

'He'll buck with me,' exclaimed Tom Dickson, looking over his shoulder. 'You snub him and I'll climb on.'

Walt settled across the cold leather and eyed his companion. 'Mister, I'm not going to snub him; either you climb up there, or you start walking. Millton's about fifty miles from here. It's your choice.'

Tom Dickson made a fierce scowl at the blood-bay, grabbed a handful of mane in his reinhand, toed in, cheeked the horse, then swiftly rose up and came down hard in the saddle.

The blood-bay stood as meekly as any old tractable cowhorse would have done.

Walt said, 'Use your knees, not your spurs, and head him southward. You know the way. You rode up it. Mister Dickson; don't gouge that horse and try to make me think he's running away with you.'

'He could run anyway,' exclaimed the tensed outlaw, intently watching the blood-bay's little pointed ears as he eased him ahead.

'He better not run,' said Walt. 'Justified or not, if he does I'm going to shoot you off his back.'

The horse did not run and he did not buck, he got a little slack in the reins, lowered his head and obediently hiked right along down the same trail he had earlier hiked up. Walt guessed that the horse had an idea he was going back to the barn where they fed hay and grain instead of washy springtime grass. Almost every horse who ever lived knew which way home was.

The cold increased, Walt suffered a little because he had nothing beneath his short jacket, but at least his hands were warm in gloves and his legs were kept warm by the sides of his horse.

The moon crossed overhead and seemed to be paling out as they crossed out of the lower meadow and headed in the direction of some old black-looking giant pine trees. Walt said, 'Bear to the left and keep away from the forest.'

They were a half mile farther along when he also said, 'Dickson; did you expect to find a road leading up to the hideout-town?'

Instead of answering the fugitive turned and cast a sardonic look back at Walt. It seemed sardonic to the deputy but maybe it wasn't; in the moonlight facial expressions were not easily read.

So far Walt had not come off very well at his ongoing interrogation, which did not actually surprise him very much. He had only asked the questions which might have satisfied some of his curiosity. The one question he had not asked was held back until they were beyond the trees and beginning to skirt an unstable section of sidehill.

'Why did you shoot that saloonman, Dickson, and after shooting him why did you drag him from the supply-room to his backbar?'

Tom Dickson rode along as though Walt had not spoken.

For a while Walt eyed the man's back, then he eased on up a little closer and said, 'Hold it up a minute,' and when the outlaw obeyed, turning in the saddle to look back, Walt walked his horse much closer and repeated the questions.

'Why did you shoot him and drag him in behind his bar?'

'How you going to prove I shot him?' Dickson asked.

'One of your horsehead rosettes was under his body. That'll do to hold you on . . . Why?'

From a fair distance behind them a horse

blew its nose with great vigour, and later Walt would think that the rider of that horse would have been angry enough to shoot the beast, except that shooting him would make things even worse. At the moment when he heard that noise, his first thought was of the Indian's horse, but if the Apache's horse had been following them they would have heard him long before this.

Walt gestured for his prisoner to rein off the trail and head for the nearest stand of tall underbrush and spindly trees. Tom Dickson obeyed, but sluggishly and as he reined off the sidehill he rode looking over his shoulder. It was this attitude which gave Walt Harney his first inkling that getting his prisoner out of the mountains and back down to Millton might not be as easy as he had thought it might be.

They reached a shielding place and sat side-by-side watching the north trail. But no rider materialized. They waited almost a full fifteen minutes, time enough for that nose-blowing horse to have passed along in their sight, and no horse or rider ever arrived.

Tom Dickson said, 'Loose animal is all. There's probably plenty of 'em up in these hills. Hell; whereever a man finds this much good feed there's bound to be livestock.'

Walt ignored most of what was being said to him. He glanced at Dickson. 'Why did you kill the saloonman?'

Dickson looked pained. 'You sure don't give up easy, do you?'

'Answer the question.'

'Deputy, you got to prove I killed *anyone,* I don't have to confess to having done it. That's how it works.'

Walt slowly shook his head. 'Not up here, it don't work like that. Not up here with just you and me, Tom.'

Dickson seemed to undergo a subtle little change as he studied the lawman. Finally he said, 'Listen; we can talk when we get down out of these hills. Get back down there in open country.'

Walt did not take his eyes off the fugitive. 'Care to have me answer that question for you?'

Dickson stared. 'You can't answer for me.'

'I'll make a stab at it. You killed the saloonman because someone told you to. Then you stole the blood-bay and high-tailed it. And Tom — somewhere behind us there is someone riding a horse that blows its nose a lot. He was looking for you; that is how you expected to reach Overman. You were going to be led there . . . Who is he, and is he the one who told you to kill Jake Sunday?'

'Jake Sunday?'

'The saloonman, and the next time you act dumb on me, Tom, or pretend you've gone deaf, I'm going to belt you out of the saddle and overhaul you on the ground . . . Isn't that it? You were supposed to meet someone up in here and he would guide you to the Overman settlement?'

Dickson was angered and sullen but he responded with a shrug and a reluctant nod of the head. 'You don't ride into Overman unless someone vouches for you.'

'Who?' asked Walt, and shifted his weight just a fraction to be light on the side of his swinging arm, something the unarmed outlaw noticed.

'My brother. Deputy, I ain't going to tell you one more damned thing no matter what you do!'

Walt listened for sounds in the ensuing silence, heard none, and decided since they could not sit forever where they were they might just as well start onward again.

'Ride out,' he said.

Tom Dickson did not look back. His mood had changed. He was no longer casual and confident. What had evidently appeared to him as a temporary inconvenience back where he had been captured, now seemed to be more menacing. He clearly did not abandon hope; Walt saw his head moving from left to right as though he expected his brother to appear any moment, but towards Walt Harney he was a lot less indulgent than he had been.

There were any number of places where the trailing man could get into position for an ambush-attempt, but in order to be successful at this sort of thing he would have to be in front and not behind, the lawman and the lawman's prisoner.

It was Walt's intention to take every precaution he could to avoid being ambushed, and to do this he intended to keep well ahead, and to change course from time to time in order to throw off the fugitive's brother.

He had no illusions, eventually they would meet, but if Walt could prevent this from happening until he and Tom were down upon the rangeland in open country where no one could approach within gunrange without courting even more risk than Walt was courting, the deputy would stop seeking to avoid the confrontation.

He finally gave Tom Dickson fresh instructions to change course, and Tom spoke bitterly over his shoulder. 'You'll never get clear, Deputy. Not of Maxwell Dickson. No one ever got clear of him unless he allowed them to. You can keep up this zigzaggin' until the cows come home and you'll never make it . . . Deputy, you still don't figure you'd be interested in working something out so's I could ride back and keep my brother from catchin' you, and you could ride on back to your town?'

Without any warning the blood-bay dropped his head and fired. If Tom Dickson had been expecting it, and if he had been an accomplished buckinghorse-rider, he might have been able to stay up there, but that was open to dispute too, because under Walt Harney's astonished eye that blood-bay horse, who hardly weighed more than nine-fifty, nearly stood on his head, then he sunfished and sucked off into a sideways spin that had Tom gasping as he grappled with both hands for anything at all he could hold tightly to.

Tom lost both buckets — both stirrups — in the first few bucks. When the horse sunfished he lost his hat and tried to shout a series of curses but the horse drove him so hard down into the saddle he could not even yell intelligibly.

Walt admired the outlaw's heroic effort to

remain across leather, but when he'd lost his stirrups, at the very best it was nothing but a matter of time and muscle, with a preponderance of both on the side of the blood-bay.

The last time he slammed into the ground then hurled himself into the air to slam down again, Tom Dickson's nose started to bleed. When the horse slammed down again, Tom lost his grips, lost his consciousness, and went off sideways striking a big pine tree — with violent force, and fell inertly in the speckled moonlight without moving again.

The blood-bay horse stopped pitching at once. He stood with his back bowed ready to resume firing if anyone climbed into the centre of his back, but when no one offered to do that, the blood-bay finally drifted over and began cropping grass.

Walt swung off and went over to pull Dickson clear of the tree and arrange his arms and legs. He was as cold-cocked as though someone had hit him over the head with a sledge. The blood was still coming from his nose, and now it was also coming from up in his hair somewhere, where his head had struck the tree.

Walt did not have good light in among the sparse old pines, but he leaned to see the fugitive's chest rise and fall, and when that did not prove entirely satisfactory either, he put a hand on the outlaw's chest — and felt the derringer under the outlaw's clothing.

Dickson's heart was still beating. In fact it was beating strongly, as though no matter what else might happen Dickson's heart would continue to beat.

Walt removed the hide-out pistol with its two-inch barrel, dropped it into a pocket and turned the unconscious man on to his stomach so that blood running from Tom Dickson's nose would not run into his throat.

Seven:
Forest Perils

The alternative to sitting there was to tie the unconscious man to his saddle and lead him down out of the trees, but of course if he were seriously injured that certainly would not help his condition.

Otherwise, Walt could simply wait; sooner or later the fugitive's brother would find them, would come stealthily over their trail when he did not see them emerge from the last section of trail he undoubtedly had seen them take.

Whatever his choice, Walt had plenty of time to decide upon it, which meant he also had plenty of time to decide that Ned's blood-bay horse was not worth shooting. No dangerously unpredictable horse was worth keeping, but this particular horse had now earned the deputy sheriff's thorough dislike.

Abandoning his prisoner, riding on down towards Millton alone, did not even cross Walt's mind although it would have been the easiest of his alternatives, simply to squatting there waiting for Tom Dickson to regain consciousness.

If it hadn't been for the secretive man on their backtrail Walt would have built a little fire to keep them both warm, would have done what he could for the injured horse-thief, and simply waited.

Except for the fire, this was exactly what he had to do while he considered the aspects of his altered condition. In the end, because he was very aware that Dickson's brother would by now perhaps have got around them on down the trail, which meant he could establish an ambush and sit there until Walt came along, it appeared clear that as awkward and trying as it would be, Walt had to start out — with his prisoner.

If he could have made a travois to drag

behind a horse with Tom stretched out upon it, there would have been a fair possibility for avoiding additional aggravation of the outlaw's condition. But that was also out of the question; Walt not only had no axe with which to cut saplings, no rope or twine to fashion the travois, but he didn't have the time either, if he intended to get southward while he still might have at least a fifty-fifty chance of remaining ahead of Max Dickson.

He knelt beside Tom and did not roll the cigarette he would have enjoyed because the scent would have travelled.

The outlaw groaned and feebly shifted his body a little. Walt bent closer and saw Dickson open his eyes. There was no clear indication that Dickson recognized the lawman leaning over him. In fact there was no clear indication that the outlaw's eyes were even focusing as he allowed them to drift, and eventually returned them to Walt's face where they remained.

Walt said, 'Can you hear me?'

The eyes did not flicker and the outlaw's face showed nothing. When Walt was about to privately decide that when his head struck that tree Tom Dickson had probably sustained a degree of serious injury, perhaps even a concussion, the outlaw weakly said,

'What in the holy hell happened?'

Walt was so relieved he smiled. 'The blood-bay fired with you,' he replied. 'Flung you head-first against the tree behind you. Cold-cocked you . . . How do you feel?'

'Half dead an' losin' ground,' muttered Dickson. 'I ache all over.' He paused a moment, weakly turned his head and said, 'Loan me your Colt for a minute. I swear I won't aim it at you.'

Walt turned. He too could see the blood-bay out there serenely cropping grass, and he sympathized, but they still had a long way to go and the blood-bay had to help them get there.

'Can you stand up?' he asked, and the horse-thief looked weakly doubtful. 'I got to lie here for a while,' he answered.

Walt of course had no idea where the injured outlaw's brother was, but he knew the man had to be close and the longer Walt sat where he was beside the horse-thief, the more imminent a meeting became.

He was satisfied that Tom Dickson could not move, and perhaps later, when Walt got him back into the saddle, he would still be incapable of making good time with Walt.

Walt's dilemma did not appear to be likely to improve favourably as time passed, but on the other hand there did not seem to be much Walt could do about it unless, as the outlaw had suggested earlier, Walt left and headed back for town without his prisoner.

As an alternative to being ambushed this began to offer Walt's sole salvation, but only providing Walt were by nature and personality susceptible to defeat, and he wasn't; in fact when he decided Tom Dickson could not be moved for a while and arose to stand gauging the surrounding night, he had selected a fresh option and when Tom Dickson closed his eyes and seemed to relax more fully on the ground, Walt took three large steps, faded out in among the old pines, and implemented his choice, which was simply not to wait, but to go head-first towards the meeting with Maxwell Dickson.

The cold seemed to be less objectionable now that he was at a lower elevation, but it was still noticeable, especially since he had no shirt beneath his jacket.

If the remaining Dickson brother was stealthily searching, and Walt was confident he must be doing so by this time, he most probably would be somewhere northward, no doubt paralleling the trail, and he would be doing it with extreme caution, for having figured out that someone had captured his brother, he would believe whoever had accomplished this, had to also be resourceful and experienced.

Walt grimaced. From here on he was going to have to demonstrate those virtues — if he could.

What particularly bothered him was the possibility that Max Dickson might slip out and around Walt, find his brother, but more important to Walt, might find the horses and either stampede them or appropriate them. Losing his prisoner would be bad, but ending up afoot in the mountains *and* losing his prisoner would be much worse.

He concentrated on making silent progress northward in among the trees where he could keep the trail in sight on his left, and at the same time not getting so far westward he would be unable to hear someone passing southward off on his right.

There was little else he could do.

The moon seemed to have nipped behind a cloud, or possibly the treetops were thicker and broader, but at any rate visibility became extremely limited. In fact as Walt moved ahead a foot at a time he could only see on both sides and directly in front for about ten or twelve yards.

He consoled himself with the thought that if *he* could not see Max Dickson, neither could Max Dickson see *him,* and since it was not to be expected that he would be manhunting, Max Dickson might not even be expecting to see anyone until he got much closer to the place where his brother was lying.

At least Walt hoped very hard this was so.

He paused often to listen. It probably should have irritated him that he was like a blindman, but being resourceful by nature he thought only about what he must do, not on what would improve his situation since obviously nothing was going to improve it.

Up ahead, but to his right, over in a generally westerly direction, there was a sound as of flowing water. It was possible the little creek he had more or less encountered up through the mountains ran over there, somewhere. He was interested only to the extent that he became oriented. Otherwise, as he continued northward, he ignored the faint sound until something like steel rattling over stones in that direction made him halt and listen.

If that had been Max Dickson's shod horse, then the horse-thief's brother was much farther eastward than Walt had thought. If it were a total stranger, which was very improbable, and traveling at night, it undoubtedly would be another candidate seeking to find the outlaw-town.

It was not an Indian because the horse was shod.

Walt decided to take a long chance and investigate. It seemed most probable to him that the shod-horse beside the creek belonged to Maxwell Dickson.

Changing course required simply facing in a fresh direction, but a couple of dozen yards in this new direction the trees thinned so much that even in the poor nightlight anyone moving across this territory would instantly be visible.

Fortunately for Walt Harney, that worked both ways. He saw the man leading his horse a step or two at a time, when the stranger turned away from the creek in the direction of shelter. Evidently the stranger had considered getting far out and around the place where Walt and Tom Dickson had disappeared in the trees, to do exactly as Walt had anticipated — establish an ambush — but now that he could see how exposed he would be, the man had decided to head back, at least in the area of the trail where he would have tree-shelter — except that Walt was already over there.

He had to allow the man leading the horse to get much closer before he could make much of an estimate about him. The stranger seemed to be about the same size and build as Tom Dickson, but he looked slightly thicker and slightly older.

He needed a haircut, Walt made out that much from a fair distance off. Also, the man wore his gun on the left rather than the right side. Left-handed rangemen or outlaws were common enough.

Walt eased his own right hand back, brushed his pistol-grip with it and waited. He was willing to bet his life this was Maxwell Dickson. In fact, the longer he stood directly in the oncoming man's way the more he actually *was* risking his life.

They were no more than fifty yards apart when Walt palmed his Colt, allowed the stranger to continue towards him another few yards, then quietly said, 'Hold it right where you are!'

The man stopped so abruptly his horse bumped a shoulder. Walt saw the left hand begin to move and offered a warning. 'Mister; you're facing one that is already drawn; you keep up that move and I'll kill you.'

Walt meant it. The man in front of him understood that Walt meant it. He pulled his left hand away, let it hang, and recovered quickly enough from being surprised to speak in an almost normal tone.

'What do you think you're doing?' he

demanded of Walt. 'I got every right to be around here.'

Walt cynically eyed his latest captive. 'Sure you have every right, and I've got your brother south of here under some trees with a bloody head — and he's got every right too.'

'What do you mean, a bloody head?' demanded the stocky man.

Walt's cynicism increased. The stranger had not denied having a brother; he had instantly revealed his interest by demanding to know more about Tom's injury.

Walt flagged with his gunbarrel. 'Drop the Colt and keep both hands in front of you. *Do it!*'

The other Dickson made no prompt move to obey but not even a simpleton pushed his luck very far when he was facing a six-gun, so he eventually lifted out the Colt and let it drop. Then he said, 'Cowboy, you're not out of these mountains yet.'

Walt palmed his badge. Dickson glanced at it but said nothing. When Walt growled and gestured for him to lead off in the direction of the southward trail Dickson obeyed without any additional hesitation. He was clearly an individual who did his thinking privately.

EIGHT:
MAX DICKSON

When they got down where Walt told Max
Dickson to tether his horse the older man
looked all around. He did not see his
brother for a very good reason, his brother
was not visible from the trail.

Later, when Walt herded his latest captive
into the gloom and pine-scented nearby
distance and they found Tom still lying
where Walt had left him, the elder Dickson
dropped to a knee, bent far over and said,
'Tom — Can you hear me, Tom?'

The younger Dickson's recovery had been
facilitated during Walt's absence just simply
by being allowed to lie still and remain
relaxed. He looked up at the anxious face
above him and spoke in a much stronger
tone than the last time Walt had heard him.

'Max; you see that blood-bay horse down
yonder? Shoot the son of a bitch.'

Maxwell Dickson looked up briefly. 'The
horse did this to you?'

'Yeah . . . Max; what about the rest of it?'

'Fine,' replied the elder Dickson, 'except
for this deputy behind me. Otherwise everything went off just fine.'

Tom leaned slightly to look around at

Walt. Then he sighed and softly frowned at his brother. 'I didn't think he could out-stalk you, Max.'

The elder Maxwell smiled mirthlessly. 'Don't mean much, Tom. He got lucky — the first time. Like I told him: He's a hell of a long way from being out of the mountains yet.'

Max raised a hand to probe his brother's head and found the clotted blood where Tom had collided with the tree. He made a clucking sound. 'Why the hell did you have to hit the tree with your *head?*' he muttered, and Tom flared out at him.

'What kind of a darnfool thing was that to say; I didn't even know he was going to buck with me, and when I sailed off I never saw no damned tree.'

Max turned, glancing upwards. 'That's a bad bump, Deputy. We got to do something.'

Walt was agreeable. 'Yeah; we got to get him down to Millton. There's a doctor down there. But until you and I had our little meeting I didn't dare strike out.' He looked at Max Dickson thoughtfully, 'Will your horse carry double?'

The elder man stiffly got back up to his feet. 'He's never been rode double.' Max pointed to his brother. 'He hadn't ought to be made to set a horse busted up like he is.'

Walt would have agreed with that, also, except that there was no other way to get Tom Dickson down out of the mountains. 'You want to leave him here?' Walt asked.

They looked at one another for a while as each one seriously considered this. Finally, Max Dickson said, 'He's a damned sight better off lyin' here. We can cover him, and I got a pony of whisky in my saddle-pockets. We can leave that with him. He'll be better off lyin' here than gettin' everything shook loose inside him tryin' to cover forty miles or so down out of the mountains.'

Walt fished forth his makings and silently worked at rolling a smoke while he pondered this idea. As he was lighting up he put a sceptical gaze upon Max Dickson; an idea had formed in the back of his mind. Earlier, he had felt positive that when Tom Dickson had killed Jake Sunday, Tom had done it because someone had told him to do it, and the main reason Walt had decided this was the case, was because Tom Dickson was a stranger around Millton, and it was highly unlikely that a pursued renegade on the run would take the time to arbitrarily hunt up someone — in this instance Jake Sunday the saloonman — and kill him for no reason.

Walt exhaled smoke, eyed Max Dickson a

while, then said, 'Why did you tell Tom to kill Jake Sunday?'

Max showed instantaneous surprise. 'He told you that?'

'Why?' demanded Walt.

'Because the son of a bitch cracked my shoulder last autumn throwin' me out of his saloon, and I'd never got a chance to get even for that. That's why.'

Walt heard Tom feebly moving behind Max and stepped sidewards. Tom was weakly groping inside his shirt. Walt fished in a jacket-pocket and held the derringer in his hand. 'Is this what you're looking for?' he asked the injured man, and turned to hurl the little weapon as far out through the darkness as he could.

Tom let his hands fall back to the ground. He had tried to use the fact that his brother was in front of him, hiding him from the deputy sheriff, and it hadn't worked. Now, he venomously said, 'You're no match for him, Deputy. You never were a match for him, neither.'

Walt finished the cigarette, ground it underfoot, ignored Tom and said, 'Okay, Max, we'll leave him here. Just you and I'll ride down to Millton. After I've got you socked away I'll come back for Tom. I think I can tool a wagon almost up this far.'

'What the hell do you want to take me to Millton for?' growled the elder Dickson.

'Being an accessory to the murder of Jake Sunday will do for openers,' replied Walt. 'Otherwise, since you been livin' up at Overman, there sure as hell is a wanted poster on you. I'll look into that too.'

Max Dickson considered the deputy sheriff for a moment. Walt was a little taller and not quite as thick as the elder Dickson. Dickson slowly reached into a trouserpocket and drew forth a flat, thick pad of notes. He looked steadily at Walt as he pitched them over for Walt to catch onehanded. 'A thousand greenbacks,' he said. 'Just get on your horse and don't look back.'

Walt felt the packet of notes, held it up where he had a close look, then he tossed them back, and from the ground the younger outlaw said, 'I could have told you, Max, you'd be wastin' your time.'

Walt gestured towards the elder man's tethered horse. Wordlessly they walked out there got the whisky bottle and walked back. Max knelt, put the bottle beside his brother and said, 'You'll be all right. Maybe you'll get a little hungry but you'll make it just fine. There'll be someone come back for you.'

Tom felt for the bottle and held it in his

hand. 'Pile some blankets on me,' he murmured.

As Max arose and turned to walk down where the other horses were, with Walt beside him, he looked worried. 'I don't like leavin' him,' he said. 'I figure he's hurt worse'n he acts like.'

Walt sympathised, but in silence. He had an extra blanket behind his saddle, handed it to Max, and as they went back he said, 'If he stays warm he'll likely make it.'

Max was not reassured. After he had covered Tom, had made him as comfortable as possible and went back with Walt to untie his horse and walk it down where Walt's animal was patiently dozing, full of upland grass, Max said, 'That gawddamned horse,' and icily eyed the blood-bay as Walt removed the saddle and bridle and left the horse free to graze. 'I'd kill him if I had a gun.'

Walt did not dissent about this nor even argue. His own opinion of the blood-bay was not much better. He said, 'Get astride and keep in front of me — and Max — if you've got a bootknife or a bellygun, I'll drop you if I see 'em.'

They started forward, angled to the trail and kept on it. Max chewed rather than smoked. While he was worrying off a corner of the plug he looked left and right, and afterwards while he was pocketing the tobacco he said, 'You won't be able to keep me locked up. No way under the sun for you to do that.'

Walt was tiring. He was also wearying of listening to remarks like this one so he rode along in total silence until, another mile along, the outlaw said, 'If the other boys back at the settlement had an inkling there was a badge-packin' lawman in their mountains . . .' Max let that trail off to be completed by the imagination of Walt Harney, but this was not the first time Walt had been in these mountains so he was not especially worried.

'Why did Jake throw you out of his saloon?' asked Walt, not just curious, but also aware that this was a subject the elder Maxwell did not enjoy. 'As a rule he only threw men out when they were drunk and troublesome. Or maybe noisy and obnoxious . . . I can picture any one of those things fitting you, Max.'

Dickson said, 'Can you,' in a voice as venomous as he could make it. 'You must have a crystal ball, Deputy, since we never laid eyes on each other before.'

Walt avoided a digression. 'Why did he throw you out?'

Dickson covered another hundred or so yards before answering. 'He was a lousy damned punkinhead, that's what your friend was, Deputy. A feller who run his saloon without no sense of humour at all . . . And I told him by gawd, when I was lyin' out there, I'd settle with him. I promised him I'd . . .'

'Hey, darn it,' protested Walt. 'All I asked was what you did to get Jake mad.'

'Nothing. Not a damned thing. I had three, four drinks and bought a bottle to take into the mountains with me. He accused me of tryin' to make trouble with some darned townsman standing alongside me at the bar; some damned spindle-tailed storekeeper, and all I did was tell the storekeeper to quit crowdin', to get back down the bar where his kind belonged and leave me plenty of room. That's all, so help me, and here come this bastard from out behind his bar with a wagon-spoke, only I didn't see him comin' in time or I could have busted his lousy skull with one shot, like shootin' a melon . . . He busted me from behind with that spoke, then, while I was dazed, he overhauled me some, and flung me out. I cracked a shoulder on a porch-post . . . Deputy, I waited a long while.'

'And when you heard Tom was coming . . . Why didn't you go back to Millton and do your own murdering?'

Max shrugged. 'What for? The kid got into trouble. He killed some Mexican's woman when she wouldn't go with him to a barn, something like that anyway, I got a letter from Tom about it, and when I wrote back I told him to head for Millton, kill that son of a bitch who owned the saloon, steal a fresh horse and head into the mountains and I'd be watching for him.'

Walt shook his head. 'Just like that. Tom didn't even know Jake. Didn't even know he was killin' the right man. He just prowled around, found the saloon, got inside and shot the first feller he met.'

'He knew,' exclaimed Max. 'I sent him a real good description.'

'And the horsehead-rosettes?' asked Walt, and drew a blank look. 'He killed Sunday in his storeroom and dragged him in behind his bar and left him there — with a glass rosette under his carcass.'

Max laughed. 'Naw; I never sent him no rosettes. If he put one under that bastard then he must have the other one to hand to me, as proof he done the killing.'

Walt, with both of those rosettes still in his pocket, did not mention them again.

'Your brother told me a Mexican was after him which was why he was in such a hurry to find you and reach Overman.'

Max did not say whether he knew this or not. All he said about it was: 'He didn't have to run from no Mex. All he had to do was pick a nice rock beside the trail, and kill the bastard when he rode by . . . But he was already on his way so there wasn't any place I could send him a letter.' Max expectorated then ran a soiled cuff across his mouth.

'He told me about the woman,' said Walt, 'but he didn't say she was dead.'

Max was not concerned about that either. 'What's the damned difference?' Then he also said, 'I was lookin' forward to seeing the kid. We hadn't been together in a long time; five or six years as near as I can recall.'

Walt rode in silence for a while, after this, thinking to himself that when they had finally met after all that time, it had been a very brief and adverse meeting. If Max Dickson had this same thought he gave no hint of it as they came down through some aspens and entered a cold big open plateau where some bedded wapiti bounded to their feet and fled in a twinkling.

Walt's horse was dragging his hind feet and he had every right; he had been going steadily since the morning before. Even the rest-halts didn't help a whole lot when there had been no supplemental grain.

Max Dickson's animal was fresher and stronger, but even so he did not act very lively as they ploughed ahead across the big meadow with its frosted grasstips and its soft scent of on onward forest.

Walt turned once to glance back. There was nothing to be seen on the backtrail nor had he expected to see anything. Tom was the only person he could imagine being interested in their progress and Tom was in no condition to arise and follow them.

The stars were crystal-clear and seemingly much larger than usual; the moon had tilted far off-centre by this time, which presaged the distant advent of dawn, but Walt did not know how much longer before sunrise and as long as he and his new prisoner could remain away from the trees and in open country he really didn't much care.

NINE:
THE FACE OF DISASTER

Walt had gone after the slayer of Jake Sunday, and he had caught him, which was all he'd intended to do, and now he was on his way back to Millton out of the mountains — with a different prisoner.

He smoked and thought of food, of his bed at the rooming-house in Millton, and eventually he also thought of the horse-thief and wanton killer he had left back yonder under some trees.

What scattered his thoughts was a brusque comment by Max Dickson. 'Someone's comin'.'

Walt watched Dickson without looking back, but Dickson had both hands in plain sight and he was also peering intently to the rear, so Walt looked back. In a moment he knew what had happened and faced forward as he said, 'It's that horse your brother stole; I guess he figures we're heading back so he's going to follow along.'

For a long while Max rode sideways trying to verify all this. He should have been able to make out a riderless horse if Walt could, and by the time Max did in fact make out the blood-bay and grunt as he straightened forward, Walt had decided that Max Dickson did not have very good eyesight.

They had a narrow ledge to pass around. The trail was no more than eighteen inches wide. On their left was a sheer stone bluff rising almost straight up. On their right the same bluff-face dropped almost thirty feet straight down where there was a little narrow ledge, then it went past this ledge and went down another sixty or eighty feet and became a blur of darkness below that.

Max swung to speak to the man behind him, inadvertently shifting all his weight in such a manner that his horse had to lurch to keep the man balanced — and his right legs both missed solid footing, soft dirt yielded, and with a mighty, terrified effort the horse heaved all his weight in the opposite direction, to the left. Max was completely un-balanced. Walt was close enough to see the look of sudden horror on his prisoner's face, then Max Dickson went off on the right side. Within a moment he was out of Walt's sight. Seconds later Walt heard an outcry, and whatever else he might have detected from below the cliff-face was lost in the sudden panic of the loose saddle-horse. Without any hesitation the horse ran ahead.

Walt could not dismount, the trail was too narrow and if he tried there was an excellent chance that he might also un-balance his mount, so he stopped, leaned out as far as he dared, seeking some sighting of Max, then eased up straight in the saddle and rode his animal on a hundred yards until they were beyond the narrow place, then he swung off, took down his lariat and hoofed it back to the place where Max had disappeared.

He called and got no response, lay prone in the dirt and projected head and shoulders out into space peering downward.

Max was lying upon the little narrow ledge with one arm and one leg dangling off it in the darkness. He was not moving.

Walt studied the man and decided that Max had probably been dazed by the fall. If, when Max recovered, he turned the wrong way, he would simply roll off the ledge.

Walt swore to himself, shook out a little loop and dangled it as best he could. But his lariat was forty feet long, to the ledge was about thirty feet, and Max's dangling leg down the far side of the ledge was another few feet, which did not leave Walt with enough slack to tie with. Still, he fished for the boot and the leg. He could not see them but he could tell each time his lariat rolled against them. He was still fishing unsuccessfully when Max groaned.

Walt called sharply to him. 'Lie still! Don't flop over on to your back or you'll slide off that ledge! Max; listen to me! My lariat is down there. If you can stand up and get the noose around you that ought to allow me enough slack to get a big knot over into the rocks, then I can probably haul you out of there.'

Dickson groaned and mumbled but offered no reply right away. Walt reiterated his warning about sliding off the ledge and evidently, as Dickson recovered from his jolt and fall, he felt around just enough to realize his very real peril.

Eventually he said, 'For Chris' sake, Deputy, help me.'

'Settle down,' called Walt gently. 'Is anything busted — an arm or a leg?'

Dickson gingerly examined himself. 'No. But my belly is sure sore; I landed on it.'

'Can you stand up?'

'I don't know . . . Hell; I only got about ten inches on this ledge, Deputy.'

Walt said, 'Try it. Stand up real easy and lean into the face of the cliff.'

'Lord . . . Hey, Deputy, I don't know whether I'd ought to or not. Can you see past me down to the bottom?'

Walt felt like swearing. 'Max, quit lookin' down. If you got to look anywhere look up. Now twist around real easy, get both feet squarely under you, and come right up the face of the rock. All right?'

'I don't know whether I'd ought to, Deputy.'

'You damned fool,' exclaimed Walt exasperatedly. 'You can lie there and starve to death if you want to. It's that or stand up so I can haul you out with the lariat.'

'. . . I'll stand up. Hey, Deputy; make that lariat fast in the rocks so'd it'll do for me to support myself with.'

Walt did that; he stood up, leaned to find a good stout crevice, knotted and re-knotted his turk's-head end of the lariat, made certain it was solid, then played out his rope until he heard Max say, 'I got it. You plumb sure it's hard and fast?'

Walt answered curtly. 'I'm sure. Max; are you afraid of high places?'

Dickson's answer was almost fervent. 'Lord yes; high places and fallin'. Always have been.'

That settled a suspicion which had been forming in Walt's mind for the past fifteen minutes. On every other subject he and the outlaw had discoursed, Max had been hard as iron.

Walt felt the rope tighten slightly as Dickson used it to support himself as he gingerly arose on the narrow little ledge. He also heard the outlaw's rasping breath. No question about it, Max Dickson had a right to be afraid, but he seemed to be closer to terror and panic than most men would have been.

Walt decided to talk Dickson into a calmer condition. 'That's a hell of a stout rope,' he called, 'and I've got it knotted into a fissure a horse couldn't pull it out of. Max, you're safe enough.'

The first indication that Dickson was indeed recovering from his panic came when his voice came up from the lower darkness with a dry question. 'You want to trade places, Deputy?'

Walt smiled in spite of himself. 'Tell me when you're ready to start climbing and I'll commence hauling you up at the same time . . . Ready?'

'Hell no; I just got standin' up. What do you expect — miracles?'

Walt waited a moment or two longer then said, 'Ready now?'

The answer was slow coming and sounded full of reluctance. 'You plumb certain about the strength of this lasso? It looks an old one to me.'

'A couple of years old is all,' stated Walt. 'Get your legs braced and take a real good grip and start walking up the cliff. All right?'

'No, it's not all right, but I can't think of no other way . . . Hey, Deputy . . . that feller my brother shot, that saloonman . . . was he a friend of yours by any chance?'

'Yeah, he was a friend — but I'm not going to cut the rope when you're halfway up, Dickson, so quit wafflin' and let's get this over with. Take hold, damn you, and start climbing!'

Dickson swore from between clenched teeth, took a solid grip, swore some more and started climbing. Walt could feel the lariat stretching under the outlaw's solid weight.

From a very great distance a wolf mournfully sang at the dying moon, which neither of the men on the little trail heeded, and elsewhere a horse picking its way down the trail towards the place where Walt was straining made the sounds a shod horse would make when he walked over stone.

Walt had no time to worry about this approaching shod horse except to suspect it would be the loose blood-bay.

He could hear the rasping loud breathing of the man out of sight over the edge of his ledge, and he could also hear small bits of shale and dirt crumbling away and falling as the straining lariat-rope chewed into the ledge-edge. No doubt but that most of that crumbling debris fell upon Max Dickson, and no doubt but that under different circumstances Max would be indignantly cursing, but right now his life depended upon holding tightly and climbing; nothing else including dirt in the face and stones on the head were likely to divert him.

For Walt, the straining was very hard. Even if he hadn't been dog-tired even before this accident he still would have found it very hard work, helping to haul a man who was about his own weight, up over the edge of the stone ledge, but being tired and worn-down after twenty-four hours of being under-fed and without rest, he was straining on spirit alone.

Finally, he saw a raw set of bruised knuckles appear, and when he dug into the rock-dust with a fresh grip on the lariat he saw the other hand also appear. He did not feel particularly triumphant, he simply began to feel relieved.

The crushed and shapeless old hat of the outlaw appeared, then the man's chalk-white face set in lines of powerful concentration.

'Keep climbing,' panted Walt. 'Don't try to grab the ledge until you're more'n half-way over it. *Climb!*'

Dickson obeyed, completely ignored the straining lawman, pulled himself by sheer power up over the lip of the ledge, balanced forward and pulled again, got most of his body upon the stone, then gave himself another hard tug and rocked forward until all his upper body fell into the dust at Walt's feet. Then, finally, Dickson relinquished his hold — with one hand — and lay in the dirt breathing like a steam-engine.

Walt stepped across the prone man, grabbed his britches and flung both legs up and around, then he stepped back and leaned against the cliff-face.

'You're beginnin' to be a trial to me,' he panted. 'Your brother wasn't nearly as much trouble.'

Still with his face in the dust Max Dickson answered. 'It ain't me, Deputy. If it'd been left to me I'd never have come within five miles of this lousy trail. Whoever told you it was fit for horseback travel anyway? If I'd fallen plumb to the bottom it would have been your fault.'

'If you'd fallen to the bottom,' replied Walt tiredly, 'it'd have solved a lot of problems for *both* of us . . . Are you all right? I mean, is anything busted like a foot or an ankle?'

The outlaw squirmed around until he could sit up with his back to the stone wall, and look outward and downward. 'Is my hair white?' he muttered.

'No, but your face sure as hell was,' replied Walt. 'Get up and let's walk on down and catch the horses.'

Max Dickson twisted to look upwards.

'Are you crazy?' he huskily demanded to know. 'I just pulled my guts out climbin' up a lousy cliff and you want to head right on out. I got to set here for a while. I'm weak as a cat.'

Walt reached, caught hold of the cloth and wrenched Dickson to his feet, pushing him against the cliff-face. 'Walk,' he ordered.

For a moment Dickson looked as though he would retaliate for being manhandled but the look in the eyes of the taller man must have discouraged this; he turned and started walking down the ledge.

Walt had to retrieve his lariat and coil it as he walked along. Behind him, the sound of shod hooves moving hesitantly down the narrow slick-rock trail started up again. He did not even look over his shoulder.

Walt's horse had been tied to a tree and Dickson's animal was standing beside the tethered animal, both of them drowsing. Dickson glowered. 'Damned horses rest while men pull their guts out.'

Walt secured the lariat, untied his horse and tested the cinch without tightening it. He rode with a loose cinch; some men did and more men didn't.

They had open country onwards ahead of them for what Walt estimated to be a mile, then there was another black wall of tall timber, but at least they were now on the downslope side of that massive rockwork hill where the dangerous trail was.

Finally, Walt called a halt and sat looking back. When the blood-bay finally appeared, and also halted to watch the mounted men, Walt grunted and gestured for Max to go forward again. He had been sure it was the blood-bay back there, but once they reached enough open territory, he had intended to make certain.

Now that he knew, he ignored the trailing saddle animal and concentrated on what lay ahead.

TEN:
TOWARDS DAWN

Up until now Walt had been too occupied to yield to his weariness but as they continued on their way through an uneventful hour of riding he began having trouble remaining awake.

He smoked and he studied the onward route with interest. He even forced himself to press a conversation with Dickson which the outlaw clearly was reluctant about. When Walt said, 'Where are you wanted?'

the outlaw answered shortly without looking back.

'What's the difference? If you figure to
make anything off me by gawd you're goin'
to have to earn it.'

'What are you wanted for?' asked Walt,
and got another cryptic retort.

'Not for messing around with some
darned Mexican's woman, you can bet new
money on that. Dumbest darned thing my
brother ever did. Except for that he wouldn't
be busted up lyin' under a tree right now,
and I wouldn't be a lawman's captive.'

'Care for a smoke?'

'Don't smoke it I chew it,' responded
Dickson, and finally twisted to scowl. 'What
you tryin' to do, Deputy, butter up to me
so's I'll tell you everything I know?'

Walt smarted a little under that remark.
'The day I'll butter up to a worthless
bastard like you, Max, they'll have icicles in
hell . . . One more question, and I think, if I
get another smart answer, I'll haul you off
that saddle and kick some waddin' out of
you.'

'Not the best day you ever saw,' crowed
the fugitive. 'Deputy, you couldn't begin to
do that the best day you ever saw.'

'The question,' stated Walt, 'is: How does
a feller reach Overman?'

Dickson laughed. 'That's something we don't have to fight over. A feller *don't* reach Overman. Not unless he's got someone up there to vouch for him.'

'All right; you already made that plain when you talked of guiding your brother up there. But how did he let you know he was on the way?'

'If you'd been listenin' you'd have known how he did that. He wrote me a letter, I told you.'

Walt nodded. 'Yeah. That's my point, Max. There's no post office for a place named Overman. Where did he write to you?'

Dickson was very slow in replying. 'He wrote and I got it, and that's all you got to know,' he eventually sullenly said.

'Naw, I got to know more than that,' stated Walt, and took down his lariat, snaked out a little loop under the baleful and apprehensive eye of his prisoner. 'I'm getting sick of you, Max.'

'What's that rope for?' growled the outlaw.

'Drop it over your head, Max, and set my horse up and yank you out of the saddle. That'll do to get you on the ground. Then I'll drag you for a spell.'

Walt hadn't sounded angry nor even agitated, and this seemed to trouble the captive more than the grisly description of what was about to happen. In a monumentally disgusted tone Dickson said, 'The mail for Overman goes to the post office in Millton.'

Walt looked sceptically at the man in front. 'I don't believe that,' he said.

'Believe it or not,' stated the outlaw. 'It goes to Leo Purdy. He either holds it until someone from Overman has to go to Millton then hands it over, or else he fetches it to a box that's cached in some rocks west of the stageroad, puts it in there, and someone from Overman picks it up on his way in.'

Walt felt like swearing. This treasure-trove of incriminating information had been passing under his nose for the Lord knew how long, and he hadn't even had a suspicion.

He knew Leo Purdy, a wispy little nondescript liverybarn dayman who had been around Millton as long as Walt had. Leo was so thoroughly colourless that in all the years he and Walt had known one another they hadn't traded fifteen words.

Max guessed his captor's reaction and laughed. With a vicious light in his eyes he said. 'Some lawman; fugitives been gettin' their mail under your nose for years. Folks in Millton had ought to get a snicker out of that.'

True enough; when the people in Harney's bailiwick heard about the mail for that settlement of outlaws passing through their own post office they were going to feel chagrined, and no doubt some of them would blame Harney; it always turned out that way: When no one else was handy, place the blame on the local lawman.

Walt strapped the lariat back to the saddle-swells and eyed his companion's saddle. 'You got any food in those pockets?' he asked, and got a negative headwag. Dickson looked disgusted again.

'I figured *you'd* have some grub,' he growled.

Walt shook his head.

'You mean you came all the way up here without figurin' on eating?'

'Didn't expect to be out of food this long,' explained the lawman. 'Figured to do about as I did — grab your brother, turn around and head back.'

'That still would have taken a full day,' protested Max Dickson. 'You didn't even bring no sardines?'

Walt ignored the comment about sardines. 'Going a day without food isn't hard, I've done it lots of times. In fact I've got a suspicion everyone might be better off if they did it once or twice a month.'

Dickson gazed bleakly at the deputy

sheriff without opening his mouth, then faced forward in the saddle and rode onward exuding contempt. Any man who would ride into the mountains the way Harney had done, with no plans except to keep going until he caught his man, earned Max Dickson's scorn.

They had to hunch against the cold as they passed steadily across fairly level broad stretches of open country, because the cold had free rein out where there were no trees to impede it.

Walt suffered and perhaps that was what kept him from dozing off. If he hadn't been a very stubborn individual they would have piled off and lit a fire to get warm by, at least until sunrise.

They eventually had no other recourse. The cold became bitter and Walt's suffering finally drove him to call a halt, and while Max held their horses, blew on his hands and stamped one foot then the other one, Walt went after kindling, got a small fire going, went after larger bits of deadfall wood, and after a short while a blazing fire was brightening the area roundabout.

Max sidled close, arms and palms extended, and said, 'Folks had ought to be able to see this for fifty miles.'

Walt was not concerned. 'Anybody's up

this time of night ought to have their heads examined.'

Max laughed, then agreed. 'Amen, brother, amen.' Then he looked worried. 'Hope my brother keeps warm enough under that blanket you pitched over him.'

Walt nodded. 'I hope so too.'

Max got out his plug and bit off a chew. 'Substitute for supper,' he explained, pouching the cud and shoving what remained of the plug back inside his jacket. 'Some of the places I've eaten in my life, chawin' tobacco was an improvement.'

'How's the grub at Overman?' asked Walt, not really interested, but curious. He opened his jacket to allow heat to reach his bare hide and the outlaw looked surprised.

'Hey; don't you own a shirt?'

'Used it to patch up a hurt hold-out I found on my way up there after your brother. You didn't answer my question: How's the grub up at Overman?'

'About like you'd expect when there's nobody up there, including a handful of squaws, who know how to cook.'

'How many people in the settlement?'

Max pondered a moment before answering. He no longer seemed reluctant to discuss the outlaw-town. 'It fluctuates; sometimes no more than ten, at other times we got maybe as many as thirty-five. Usually during the winter we got more; summertime when fellers go down along the stageroads and towns to make a livin', we got less.'

Walt closed his jacket and buttoned it. 'Where exactly *is* Overman? I know it's in the mountains, and they tell me it's northwest of Millton, but how far from Millton is it?'

'Hell of a ride,' stated Dickson, and pointed. 'If the light was better you'd see a spiky sort of pinnacle yonder to the west. The settlement is directly below it on this side of the rims, in a hell of a fine big meadow with a waterfall behind the town against the mountains.' Max let his arm fall to his side. 'There's some mighty nice log cabins up there, and a blacksmith's shop, an' a gunsmith's place. Once, we even had a doctor; he was a feller from Montana who loaded some redskins with laudanum and operated on them. They died . . . The Doc was drunk as a lord when he did that, and the law got after him. But he hasn't been up there now for three, four summers. Last I heard he was respectable as all get-out and had a regular carriage-trade down in Denver.'

Max spat into the fire, stepped back

slightly because of the growing flames and heat, studied Walt for a while then also said, 'The place is located so's can't no one come on to it without bein' seen for a mile first. Deputy, if you'd managed to follow me and my brother up there . . .' Max drew a rigid forefinger across his own throat. 'The others would have spotted you and set up an ambush. It don't happen often, but in the length of time I been wintering at Overman I've seen it done a couple of times. Once it was a federal marshal.'

Walt looked across the dancing fire. 'They killed a federal marshal?'

'Naw; they ambushed him before he seen the settlement, knocked him over the head and packed him clean across the rims and two-thirds of the way down the opposite side and left him. He never come back. We always figured he was either smart enough to know we was being nice *that* time, or else the knock on the head fixed him so's he couldn't remember where he'd been. Anyway, we watched for two weeks, but he never come back.'

Walt smoked and thought, weighed all he had been told and speculated that someday he would like to ride up there and see the place, not necessarily like a knight in shining armour on a mission of righteousness, but just to see what an outlaw-settlement actually looked like. He had heard of other such settlements, almost invariably long after their demise either through attacks by posses, or simply by being abandoned. There were also legends of these places which had sprung full-grown from someone's fertile imagination and in fact the first few times he had heard of Overman he had thought it was one of these places.

'For that many renegades in one place,' he told Max, 'we sure don't have a lot of lawlessness around here.'

'That's one of the rules,' explained the outlaw. 'No one is to steal a horse, rustle no cattle, rob no bank nor store nor stage.'

'Your brother didn't keep your law,' said Walt drily. 'You told him to kill a man and steal a horse.'

Max shrugged. 'I never said it *couldn't* be done. I said it *wasn't supposed* to be done. That way, Overman and his councilmen figured you'd let them be. They told us that's how those things worked and it was all right with us. After all, we was protected and safe; obeyin' a few simple rules was no sweat.'

'No, of course not,' replied the lawman drily, 'as long as you felt like obeying them. Who is Overman?'

'The feller who built the settlement, who owns it now and who still runs it, even from his wheelchair.'

'He's crippled?'

'Yeah. Got shot through the body during a bank robbery in Montana. Ever since, he's been settin' down. Can't use his legs. Can't even stand up, and over the past couple of years he's been lookin' thinner and paler. My guess is that he's just about ready to cash in. Meanwhile, though, it's his town and he's got a couple of real fast gunhands to keep order for him.'

Walt dropped his smoke into the fire. 'Damnedest thing I ever heard,' he muttered.

Max shrugged again.

Off in the east there was a cold streak of pale light inches above a ragged horizon. The new day was shortly to arrive. Neither of the men were anxious to resume the ride because the moment they walked away from their fire the cold would close around them again in a frigid hold.

Max eventually said, 'Deputy; too bad you work for the law. You'd be the kind of a feller a man would like to ride the rims with.'

Walt raised tough eyes. That had been a compliment and he had accepted it as such. 'Max; you're a no-good son of a bitch,' he replied casually, 'but I suppose if a man didn't care about riding with one, he could do worse.'

Dickson laughed, spat again, looked all round, looked back at the fire and turned to get his backsides warm. That was the major drawback to a roaring blaze on an icy pre-dawn morning; it never warmed but one half a person at a time and while that half was warming the other half was freezing.

Eventually, not at all pleased, Walt said, 'Get your seat warm then climb into the saddle.'

They scuffed dirt over the fire until it was smoking only, then they struck out again. Walt decided to turn off eastward; he knew where a settler had a claim back in the wooded foothills, and Walt was hungry enough to eat the skirts off a sweaty saddle.

Max did not question their route. He probably did not know they were digressing from the route on down to Millton. Whether he had known or not would have had no effect. Walt expected to scent woodsmoke by the time they left the worst of the mountain-trail and angled over where someone with a very sharp axe and a very strong back had been felling timber to sell wood down at Millton, while at the same time clearing land for grass and grain.

By the time Max wrinkled his nose and said, 'By gawd, Deputy, I smell stove-smoke and fresh coffee,' Walt had already seen the little steady light out through the trees. His acquaintance the settler was evidently up and stirring.

'Straight onward,' he told Dickson. 'You'll see the log house directly. If you mind your manners maybe we'll get some of that coffee.'

ELEVEN:
A RESPITE

The settler was a tall, rawboned greying man who seemed as a result of having been by himself so much of the time to be unwilling to talk much. When he saw Walt and his prisoner come out of the westward trees and ride across his clearing, the settler reached inside his door and brought forth a rifle. He leaned on it, motionless, and when Walt was recognizable the settler still did not relinquish his rifle but he seemed to relax a little. And he nodded when Walt drew rein and said, 'Morning, Turner. This is Max Dickson, a prisoner. We smelled that boiling coffee a mile off. Mind if we dismount?'

The settler didn't mind, but he studied

Dickson with steady interest as he continued to stand in silence, eyeing his visitors. 'Climb off,' he said. 'The coffee's about ready.' As the mounted men stiffly got down the settler shifted position a little and gazed back towards the pink-tinted far-away peaks. 'Where was he, Walt — Overman?'

'No; not when I got him, Turner, but he'd come from there, and we left his brother on the trail to Overman lying under a tree back yonder.'

The settler was interested. 'Hurt?'

Max said, 'Damned horse flung him into a tree.' Max looked over his shoulder. 'That lousy horse has been following us. Blood-bay, not real big. If you see him, Mister, shoot the son of a bitch and do all mankind a favour.'

Walt gestured. 'This is Max Dickson. That there is Turner Martin.'

Max looked, and looked away. Turner nodded gravely, then led the way to his log barn where the saddle animals could be cared for, and afterwards he led them back to his warm, weather-tight log house. It was not large, but there were three rooms, two of which looked as though they had been added on long after the main large room had been erected.

The coffee was fresh and black, and strong

enough to melt lead. They drank it listening to the fire crackling in Turner Martin's big iron stove, and Martin completed his slow study of Dickson before turning to the stove to pitch several more pieces of dry bread into his big iron skillet.

He had maple syrup, which was a rarity; very few people knew there were any maple trees in that part of the country.

Walt and his dirty, unshaven and sunken-eyed prisoner succumbed to the heat. They were tucked up and tired men, hard as nails otherwise they would have caved in long ago. Turner Martin, who always managed to be busy and to say nothing unless words were pulled out of him, made an ample platter of fried bread to eat with the maple syrup, and motioned his guests to the table as he poured coffee into three cups.

Walt was ravenous. He ate until Turner Martin put a doubtful gaze upon him and gently shook his head. But he kept frying more bread.

Dickson was also hungry, but after a while he concentrated less on food and more on the coffee, which he said was very good. It wasn't, except by the standards of a man who had almost never in his entire lifetime tasted really good coffee.

Once, Max Dickson shot his host a secretive look and Walt saw this and wagged his head at the fugitive. 'Don't be foolish,' the deputy said without particular rancour. 'Drink your coffee and be content, Max.'

It was good advice. By the time Walt was ready also to sit back their host had fried his own breakfast, had brought the laden platter to the table and had got comfortable. He smiled at Dickson.

'If you want help, you'll have to get it somewhere else,' Turner Martin quietly said, and picked up his eating utensils. 'My wife was killed in a stage robbery.'

Dickson turned slowly towards his captor and Walt looked back at him without speaking. Clearly, whatever hopes the outlaw might have entertained when he had arrived at this clearing, they were not now as strong as they once had been.

Turner finished eating and arose to clear the table. As he passed behind Dickson he said, 'Deputy; you're worn down to a nubbin'. I'll chain this feller in the barn and keep an eye on him if you'd like to get a few hours of sleep.'

Walt would have liked nothing better but instead of accepting the offer he simply crookedly smiled, walked to a window to look out into the brittle cold morning, and to decline the offer with thanks. Behind him, the prisoner also casually arose to stretch — then to whirl in a blur of movement and lunge for the holstered Colt dangling from a wall-peg near the front door of the cabin.

Walt was at the opposite side of the room; he turned at the sudden sounds of action but there was no way he could have crossed to the front door. Turner Martin could. He was already closer to the door where he was standing by the stove, and despite his silence, his almost stolid look, he could move with astonishing haste. He did it now, the moment instinct told him what the outlaw was trying to do.

They met at the doorway, both straining very hard, one to reach the holstered gun the other man seeking to prevent the gun from being yanked from its holster.

Walt whirled, right hand dropping to his hip, but they were already across the room, both men crushing together in their desperation, two strong hands and arms raising in a blur towards that dangling sixgun.

Max got the gun but Turner Martin's powerful right hand closed vice-like around Dickson's wrist holding Max motionless. He could not draw the weapon. He launched his body sideways to strike Martin, to perhaps knock him away, and Martin did not budge.

Max tried striking viciously with his left fist, and missed, so he swung his body to ram his knee upwards too, but this time Turner Martin only had to shift position a little to take the blow on the upper thigh rather than in the groin.

Now, Turner, the man who had been cutting and splitting wood, who had been grubbing out tree-stumps and working up the tangled virgin soil, stopped being defensive and turned on Max Dickson with a low growl. Evidently that knee to the thigh had been painful.

Turner reached with his free hand, caught hold of the outlaw's jaw from below the chin and began to inexorably bend Dickson's head back.

Walt, who could not have fired even if he had wanted to, started forward, then stopped.

Dickson's head went slowly but steadily backwards. He fought hard to prevent being bent backwards but Turner Martin was a very strong man. Finally, Max relinquished his hold on the holstered sixgun, jumped back as far as he could to get enough leeway to bring his head down, and as he did this he aimed a savage blow.

Turner had seen the shift coming, had also let go of the outlaw's wrist and had whirled to keep the pressure on Max, but when the fist came, Turner was not quite prepared to avoid it. He took the blow on his lowered head, having at the very last moment seen what was coming and having hunched his shoulders at the same time he hid his face. The blow landed savagely and squarely. Turner's knees sprang outwards a little and his hand under the outlaw's jaw loosened. In a twinkling the outlaw jumped still farther back, saw the temporarily stunned condition of his host, and was leaning to hurl himself towards the gun again when Walt reached from behind and half spun the outlaw off-balance.

Walt was there, waiting, when Max turned, caught himself and raised both arms. Walt went in with a pawing left hand, fired his cocked right fist over the outlaw's guard and caught Dickson flush up alongside the head.

Max almost fell. He in fact staggered into Turner Martin and that was his fatal error. The woodcutter had almost completely recovered from being struck in the head. He measured Max, came about almost lazily on the balls of his feet and sledged a bony right fist into Dickson's temple.

The outlaw collapsed like a wet sack.

Walt, ready to strike again, had to lean back to regain a normal balance, and afterwards to drop his arms. Turner gently wiggled the hand he had cold-cocked the outlaw with. His face clearly reflected the pain of that powerful strike against Dickson's skull.

Walt was apologetic. 'I wouldn't have stopped if I hadn't been about used up. I'm sure sorry this had to happen.'

The settler eyed the man on the floor. 'Damned fool,' he grumbled, and raised smoky eyes. 'Care for another cup of coffee?'

They returned to the stove and because Walt felt an obligation to the woodcutter he told him the entire story, from the time Ned had lost the horse, and the killing of Jake Sunday had been discovered right up until the moment he had ridden out of the forest with Max Dickson.

Turner's comment was: 'I guess their way of makin' a livin' is better than my way. At least they get more money and don't have to work so hard — but seems to me it'd be kind of hard to sleep at night.'

Walt smiled crookedly. 'Not to that kind. They sleep like babies. I've had 'em in my jailhouse still with the blood on their shirt-fronts, and they eat a big supper then drop right off to sleep.'

Turner looked down again. 'Well; I'll chain him, and you might as well get some rest too.'

Walt hadn't approved of the idea earlier, but now he did. But he waited until his host returned from the barn with his log-skidding chains, then Walt supervised the securing of his prisoner and only after he was confident Max Dickson could not possibly free himself did Walt head for the loft out back.

He was afraid that once he slept he might not awaken until the following day, so he asked Turner Martin to rouse him by early afternoon. The woodcutter agreed, but he said, 'There's no big hurry, Walt. If you don't reach town until tomorrow it's not going to make any difference is it? Then why not sleep as long as you need to, and afterwards we'll eat supper tonight, maybe play a few hands of twenty-one, and in the morning you can strike out.'

Walt offered no argument. He simply smiled and reiterated his wish to be awakened in early afternoon, then climbed the loft ladder, burrowed into the fragrant timothy hay up there, kicked out of his boots and slowly relaxed.

It was warm upstairs in the log barn. Sunshine beating on the roof had made the loft almost as warm as the house had been.

While he awaited sleep Walt thought about all the things which had happened to him since he'd left town the day before; more than usually happened to someone in a week.

He wondered about the younger Dickson. By now he had perhaps recovered sufficiently to sit up and perhaps build a small fire to keep warm by. It occured to Walt that even without a saddle animal the young Dickson might still head for the outlaw-settlement. He doubted that Dickson could make it that far through the mountains on foot, weak and bruised, before Walt could return to re-capture him, unless of course Dickson could find either another horse, or perhaps one of the men from the settlement who would help him.

If he got to Overman, Walt's chances of taking him into custody again would be considerably diminished. On that, he finally fell asleep, and his final thought on the subject was that he really wanted young Dickson; not for stealing Ned's worthless blood-bay gelding, but for killing Jake Sunday. For that wanton murder Walt wanted Tom Dickson more than he wanted his brother, or, for that matter, more than he had ever before wanted a fugitive.

Twelve:
News from the Apache

When Turner roused Walt in the lazy heat of early afternoon and waited until Walt had pulled on his boots, it appeared that the woodcutter was a little preoccupied.

As they desended the ladder and walked out of the barn into brilliant sunshine, Turner said, 'He offered me two thousand dollars to unlock the chains. All I had to do was let him take his own horse and my sixgun.'

Walt eyed the settler. 'That's a lot of money.'

Turner agreed. 'With that much money . . . But would I have been able to spend it?'

'No; the minute you handed him your loaded Colt you'd have found out. Well hell — otherwise, how is he?'

'All right. I fed him again, gave him some branchwater with whisky in it, let him shave with my razor, and wash out back the house.'

When Walt reached the porch and saw the man chained out there, he decided that his prisoner looked a whole lot more present-able then *he* looked.

Turner was willing to lend Walt his razor

too, but Walt settled for hot water to wash in, and afterwards he even declined the offer of food, then waited until Max had the chains removed, and herded him to the barn where their rested horses waited.

Walt let the prisoner do all the saddling and bridling. Walt tried discreetly to pay Turner but the woodsman would accept nothing. 'If he's a stagerobber, just make darned sure he hangs,' was all Martin said.

Later, when they were leaving the yard, Martin nodded to the outlaw and saluted Walt with a smile and a hand-wave. They were a half mile onward before the prisoner said, 'You had a lot of nerve, leavin' me in the house with that crazy devil. He just sat there and stared; it gave me the creeps.'

'Sure,' agreed Walt sarcastically, 'but it didn't stop you from offering to pay him to turn you loose.'

Dickson looked around. 'Well. What did you expect? The closer I get to your town the worse off I get.'

Walt looked back, saw nothing, not even any sign of the blood-bay, and settled forward with a yawn and a loud sigh.

They had a fair share of riding ahead of them. By his best guess they should be on the outskirts of Millton by late evening. He had a smoke, watched Max worry off a chew, and finally turned lazily and for no particular reason to look back.

There was a rider coming. He was travelling inexorably in their direction and he was alone. Walt's comfortable lethargy fell away at once. For a while, Max Dickson did not turn in the saddle, so he did not know they were being followed.

Finally, when it appeared certain that the man back yonder was not just some inadvertent traveller, but that he was seeking to over-take the pair of men up ahead, Walt decided to conclude the chase quickly.

He called to Max. 'Get off your horse.'

The outlaw turned, baffled by the order, and saw that distant rider. For a long time he rode along staring back there, but when Walt repeated the order Max drew rein and swung to the ground.

Walt pointed. 'Now take off the saddle and bridle.'

Max stared. 'Take them off . . . ?'

'You're going to hoof it from here on.'

Max spluttered. 'What the hell are you . . . Are you out of your head? Hoof it — why?'

'Because I'm going back to meet that rider, and I'm not going to leave you down here on a horse, unguarded. Now hurry up; strip the horse and turn him loose.'

It took more time for the full significance of all this to reach Max's mind and be interpreted back into action, but the moment Walt reached for his hip-holster the outlaw began profanely to remove the riding equipment.

Far back, the oncoming rider slowed his horse to a steady walk. He seemed very interested in what was going on ahead of him, and finally, when he saw Max slap his horse on the rump to start it towards Millton by itself, the distant rider stopped altogether and sat back there, not comprehending at all.

Walt turned back. As he did so he said, 'Max; sit down and wait. If I don't come back you'll be better off than if I do. If you try to run, out here on this open rangeland, I'll catch you no matter how fast you are.'

Walt rode back towards the distant rider at a slow lope. When he had the man well in sight he drew his Colt and continued with it lying in the saddle-seat out of sight. He was crossing a vast expanse of open country. The other man seemed unwilling to come any closer, but neither did he seem inclined to retreat. Walt was only a few hundred yards distant when the other man slowly raised a thick, stubby arm above his head, palm forward.

It was an Indian!

Walt slowed his horse and tipped down his hat to get a better sighting, but even then, not until he was within pistol-shot did he recognize the hold-out. It was the youthful bronco he had patched up at the creek, using his shirt to make a decent clean bandage.

The Indian lowered his arm and sat like a stone carving until Walt was close enough to discern that the bronco had his entire upper body bandaged beneath a polka-dot shirt.

Walt holstered his Colt and called ahead in border-Spanish. 'What passes, friend?'

'Much passes,' responded the Apache, a trifle drily Walt thought as he urged his horse the last few yards then halted again.

'I didn't think you'd be able to ride,' Walt told the bronco. 'You shouldn't have tried it, either.'

The Indian ignored all this to say, 'You left a man lying under a tree.' He reached inside his shirt and drew forth a Colt six-gun which he offered to Walt butt-first. 'This is the gun of that man.'

Walt accepted the weapon without examining it. He did not in fact take his eyes off the Apache because he was beginning to have a premonition.

'He is dead,' said the hold-out, and because this was exactly what Walt had just begun to suspect this was why the hold-out had trailed him so long, Walt simply looked back at the Indian and inclined his head.

'Broken inside,' said the Apache. 'Our doctor came down and looked at him. Our doctor said he bled to death on the inside.'

Walt sighed and turned his head. Max Dickson was doing exactly as Walt had suggested, he was sitting out there on the grass, small and insignificant in the middle distance. 'That's his brother,' Walt told the Indian. 'He's from the renegade-town up against the far foothills.'

The Apache looked gravely down through the dancing afternoon heat. 'What do you want us to do with the dead one?' he asked, still squinting out at Max Dickson.

Walt didn't think it mattered very much once a man was dead, what people did with him. He also knew that Apaches seldom dug graves for people who were not of their own clans, so he said, 'There are plenty of crevices back there.'

The Indian nodded his head. 'And his blanket?'

It was Walt's blanket. 'Keep it, and anything else you want. But make sure you give him a good burial in the mountains.'

The Indian turned slowly towards Walt. 'I'll take care of that. I owe you that much . . . Anything else?'

While they were looking at one another Walt had an idea. He handed back the dead outlaw's gun, the Colt which had been used to kill Jake Sunday, the gun Tom Dickson was wearing when he was trying his hardest to reach sanctuary.

'One more thing,' said Walt. 'Do you know where the renegades have their village?'

'We have spied on it many times,' replied the hold-out.

'. . . Burn it!'

The Apache blinked, which was the only surprise he allowed himself to show.

'Set it afire in the night and burn those men out of there,' he said.

The Indian remained silent for a time. He was not nonplussed, he was simply considering the lawman's proposition. After a while he made a confession. 'We have talked of doing that many times. The reason we did not do it was because we thought posses and the army would come.'

'No posse will come from Millton,' stated Walt, 'and there is no army post closer than Huachucha. Burn it.'

The Apache continued narrowly to eye Walt for a moment longer then he whirled his horse and loped towards the distant protective shelter of the forest-fringe lying a mile or two west of Turner Martin's place.

Walt watched for a while then turned southward riding at a walk. He did not particularly like his new obligation of telling Max Dickson that his brother was dead. He did not like Max and he had not liked his brother, but when it came down to the total finality of death a lot of men who were unshakable in their disapproval of other men, hesitated; right now Walt Harney was one of these men.

But Max made it a little easier. As soon as Walt was close enough the outlaw arose from the warm earth and pointed. *His* horse had not even looked back on his rush southward in the direction of town, but the blood-bay was out there a couple of hundred yards grazing and keeping an eye on the men. He was clearly one of those horses who out of preference remained where people were.

'I ain't going to ride that son of a bitch,' Max said.

Walt looked elsewhere. 'Your horse is plumb out of sight,' he murmured, and that set Max off again.

'Off course he's out of sight! It was your silly idea to make me turn him loose, wasn't it! Well, what did you expect?'

Walt looked out where the blood-bay was gazing over at them, and took down his lariat. 'I'll fetch him back,' he told Max and reined away under a shower of fierce imprecations and stout refusals by Max Dickson that he would have anything to do with the blood-bay.

Walt didn't have to chase the gelding. He was poised to, had his rope ready and his spurs turned to rake his animal's ribs, but the blood-bay stood as docilely as a pet-raised horse. Walt dismounted, talked his way up, eased the rope into place and turned back to mount up and lead the blood-bay back where Dickson's mound of saddlery was lying. He tossed the tag-end of his rope to the man on the ground and gave an order.

'Saddle him up — or turn him loose and start walking. Either way we can't make it to town until evening, but on foot you're goin' to be bad off by the time we get there.'

That was the plain truth and Dickson knew it as he held the lariat looking balefully down it at the serene-looking little blood-bay horse. Then he started down the rope with his bridle, softly talking to the blood-bay. Fortunately, horses went by the *sound* of a man's voice not the words.

But there was no need to go through the bronco-routine. The blood-bay stood as quietly to be rigged out as though he were someone's pet, and in fact he may have been at one time, until his unpredictable disposition made enemies for him out of former friends.

When it was all finished Max Dickson stood off and stared at the horse. Finally he said, 'The bastard's thinkin'. He's schemin' which way he's goin' first and what tricks he's goin' to uncork on me.' Dickson looked over at Walt. 'You act as pick-up-man,' he growled, and jerked his hat down as he resolutely turned and marched back, turned the gelding twice, then cheeked his way up across saddle-leather.

The horse simply stood there waiting meekly to be guided. Walt sighed and said, 'Not now. He's not going to do anything right now.'

They started southward. The heat may have had something to do with it; for a fact as the two men rode down through it they felt the loosening of night-knotted muscles. There were no trees to impede the steady burn of sunlight, for a change. Maybe the horse felt the same way; too comfortably hot and relaxed to be difficult, but whatever his reason he plodded along without even turning his ears back, and Max eventually let up on keeping an intent vigil. He even gnawed on his chewing plug and rode along within a few yards of Walt looking almost pleased.

But they were both horsemen, which meant that they had no illusions. Sooner or later, when whatever it was which triggered the blood-bay occured, the little horse would explode.

Walt only hoped he would not do it until they reached town and could get clear of him. Max may have wished the same thing, but for Max, reaching Millton didn't mean the same thing it meant for Walt.

The deputy was rolling a smoke, with both reins looped, when he said, 'Max; your brother died last night.'

The outlaw did not draw rein, he did not even slacken the rhythmic movement of his jaws. He turned his head though. 'That feller who rode up behind you bring that message?' he asked.

Walt lit up and blew smoke before replying. 'Yeah. That was the Apache I patched up with my shirt. He found Tom under the tree — dead . . . Max, it must have been something more than the crack alongside the head.'

'Internal,' agreed the elder outlaw. 'Oh

hell; he was pretty young for dyin'.'

Walt said nothing. No one was ever too young for dying. A man died when he was supposed to die, young, old or in between.

Max said no more. They had Millton in sight by the time shadows were forming and near-night was descending along the far slopes.

Something inside Max Dickson seemed to be shrivelling, to be atrophying, but until they were on the outskirts of town Walt had no inkling his companion was undergoing a change.

'The whole gawddamned thing is pointless,' Max said quietly. 'From beginning to ending, from birth to death the whole silly damned business don't have a single decent reason . . . Deputy?'

Walt shrugged. He was no philosopher, he was simply a deputy sheriff paid to do his job.

'The coyotes and wolves will get him,' Max said.

'Naw; I let the hold-out keep the blanket and gun, to give him a decent burial.'

Up ahead, they heard a dog barking, a cow lowing, and someone loudly whistling out behind a shed on the east side of the road-way as they entered town.

Thirteen:
Welcome Back!

Millton was one of those places which had been so well established for so long, that even on the frontier it had habits; when the local deputy sheriff rode down to his jailhouse building at suppertime, not a soul who would have recognized him saw his passage, but later, after he had locked Dickson into a cell and was leading the two drawn-out horses down to the liverybarn, old Ned Allen was emerging from the cafe upon the opposite side of the road loudly sucking his teeth, and stared.

Ned rarely hastened but this evening he did, and managed to reach the runway of his barn just as the nighthawk was climbing down off the ladder he used to light the runway overhead lamp with. The nighthawk took those two travel-stained horses without a word.

Ned bustled up with a loud exclamation. 'By gawd, Walt, you done it! Sure as I'm standing here you brought back my blood-bay!'

Walt continued to watch the nightman leading the animals away for a moment before he turned to face the liveryman and

say, 'What the hell are you acting so surprised about?'

Ned's enthusiasm wilted. 'Well; I didn't
mean I never expected you to fetch him
back. That's not what I meant at all.'

'You sure sounded exactly like that's what
you meant,' growled the dirty, rumpled,
unshaven and villainous-looking lawman.

'No. Come on, Walt, you know me better'n
that. Listen, if you hadn't never brought the
darned horse back I'd never have . . .'

'Did you know that darned blood-bay
don't only pitch under a cold blanket, Ned?'

'No. Does he?' Enquired the older man,
widening his gaze with too much innocence.
'I only got him in a trade a few days before
he was stolen, Walt.' Ned had an idea and
his face brightened. 'Anyway, whatever his
fault he brang back your outlaw didn't he?'

'He *killed* my outlaw, Ned! He flung him
against a pine tree and busted him inside
and he died last night.'

'Oh Lord! Really? Was that the feller who
stole the blood-bay, then?'

'And who also killed Jake,' replied Walt.

Ned stared a moment before his eyes
turned narrow again. 'Then who rode him
back tonight?'

'Another outlaw,' said Walt, and turned to
depart. 'Tell your nighthawk to cuff my

horse good, and grain him, and see that he's got plenty of meadow-hay and plenty of flesh bedding. All right?'

Ned nodded. 'Sure. You don't have to tell us to look after your animal, Walt.'

'I told you all the same,' growled the law-man and hiked back up in the direction of his office, except that two-thirds of the way along he crossed over towards the lighted cafe with its invitingly steamed windows and orange lampglow.

Ned remained in place until his nightman came forth and said a little timidly, 'What in hell's wrong with the deputy, Mister Allen?'

Ned turned with a flash of anger. 'Nothing's wrong with the darned deputy, Reg. You get your blasted tail back in there and cuff his horse good, and grain it and make certain the bedding is fresh. You understand?'

The nightman had already retreated long before Ned's tirade had ended.

The preacher came along, walking gravely up through the warm evening from the lower end of town. He had seen Walt depart from the liverybarnyard and now, seeing Ned still out there, veered inward. Ned turned waspishly to glare, but Preacher Bruce Frisby was a bull of a man; Ned had once seen him wade through the crowd at Jake's saloon to collar a man who had just been paid on Saturday night and who was getting ready to drink it all up, knock several heads together and haul the man with the money outside and drag him all the way to the man's own front porch, and slam him against the wall down there with a big fist under his nose.

That time, even Jake Sunday had not opened his mouth.

Now, Ned's slow anger was still simmering but all he said when Bruce Frisby asked whether or not that hadn't been Walt Harney, was: 'Yas; and it sure as hell wasn't Santa Claus.'

The hulking preacher turned a mild look. 'What does that mean, Ned?'

'He's in a vile frame of mind. Maybe it's because that horse of mine he went after bucked an outlaw off and hurt him. I don't know. Except that he's sure not as pleasant as he usually is.'

'Been several days on the trail,' said the minister in that same mild tone of voice. 'That's always hard on a man.'

Bruce nodded and strode ahead, on up through the settling night. Ned gave it up with a curse, a big sigh and a momentary rolling upwards of the eyes, then he went in the direction of his barn runway.

Walt was having difficulty manipulating the tray of food from the cafe, and the door of his jailhouse, when Preacher Frisby walked up and reached to shove the door inward, and smile. 'You smell like a billy goat,' he said, and followed Walt inside still smiling.

Walt said, 'Did Jake get a good burial?'

Bruce Frisby closed the door gently. 'Best turn out I ever saw, Walt. Surprisingly enough there were womenfolk there; my ladies of the Altar Society in their choir robes came and sang. It was an amazing crowd. Even the cowmen came from miles around. I had no idea . . . Well, of course I knew a lot of men liked Jake, but I also had heard over the years a lot of people didn't like him, as well.'

Walt pointed. 'Open the cell-room door, will you, Bruce?'

The preacher obliged, then followed Walt down where a guttering old smoky lamp was burning, and leaned to look in at Max Dickson when Walt shoved the tray of food beneath the steel-strap door.

Bruce said, 'Him . . . ?'

Walt shook his head as he straightened up. 'Naw; this is Maxwell Dickson, brother of Tom Dickson. It was Tom who killed Jake

— by order of this one — and it was also Tom who stole the blood-bay horse from Ned — and the horse killed Tom up in the mountains . . . I'll tell you the whole story another time, Bruce.' Walt faced the man he had shared some hair-raising adventures with coming down out of the mountains. 'Max . . . you got tobacco?'

Dickson had enough. 'Sure, plenty. But I sure need a big guzzle of whisky, then fifteen hours of sleep.' Max stared at Walt a long while, as though the minister were not also outside in the corridor beyond his cell. 'Deputy; I'm not hung yet.'

Walt nodded and turned to lead Bruce Frisby back up to the office. There, he dug around in a wall-cupboard until he found a bottle of whisky which had about a quarter of its original contents still inside. He said, 'Sit down, Bruce, I'll be right back,' and returned to the cell-room. As he shoved the bottle through the steel straps he said, 'Max, if you're still drunk in the morning I'll bring in buckets of cold water and fling them over you.'

Dickson held aloft the bottle and squinted. 'What the hell do you think I am — a darned schoolboy!' He turned his back and allowed Walt to get almost up to the corridor doorway before he also said, 'Hey,

Deputy — thanks.'

Bruce Frisby cocked a quizzical eye as Walt returned to the office, kicked the cell-room door closed and dropped the oaken bar into place in its steel hangers, then walked to his table to ease wearily down and pitch aside his hat.

'What are you staring at?' he demanded.

'You,' stated the preacher forthrightly. 'Since when do you give them liquor in the jailhouse?'

'Since this evening, when I had to tell him his brother died last night,' replied Walt, leaning back and hoisting booted feet to the table-top. 'His brother was a no-good murdering, horse-stealing son of a bitch, Bruce, and that's not strong language. That's the *best* I can say about him. Anyway — that one in the cell didn't think so, and it cut him down to beat hell to hear that his brother had died up there in the mountains trying to find Max. So; he'll get half-drunk tonight. That's all the whisky there is in that bottle . . . Bruce; I'll tell you straight out — he *should* want you to sit in there with him while he talks it out, but he doesn't know how to talk it out. He knows how to get drunk though.'

Frisby said, 'That's two-thirds of it, isn't it? Two-thirds of them are like that, Walt, and the Lord knows how they end up like that.'

Walt sighed and arose. 'I'm hungry and tired. Care to came over to the cafe with me?'

Frisby also arose. They went out front upon the plankwalk and separated, Preacher Frisby up in the direction of his rectory, Deputy Walt Harney across the road to the cafe where he had only a half hour earlier got the tray for his prisoner.

Around them both, belated information was being dispensed but in general, because many people were preparing to retire this soon after supper, it would not become common knowledge until after breakfast in the morning that Walt Harney had brought back an outlaw — not the one he had gone after, but another outlaw.

The cafeman, who was an old friend, studied Walt's face and decided not to ask questions. Otherwise, perhaps because it was a little late for most of the local people — mostly single men — who ate at the cafe, to be on hand, the place was almost empty as Walt sat slowly eating, and drinking coffee, and thinking back in silence.

There was a bearded stagedriver wearing a long coat and a muffler, things which suggested he would be driving through the night, but he did not even know who Walt Harney was.

There was also a stranger, a man who had arrived in town only this very morning, and who Walt would eventually get to know and like; he was Jake Sunday's nephew and heir, a florid big good-natured man named Morgan Sunday. He had heard of the murder of his uncle several days earlier. He was not in town, now, so much to inherit as to see what could be done about catching his uncle's killer.

Walt saw those two and did not remember either of them ten minutes later. By the time he finished eating and arose to spill silver coins beside his place, the other two men had already departed.

Walt and the cafeman exchanged a look. The latter said, 'Get some sleep,' and turned away.

Outside the night was beginning to cool-out, like a carcass. Walt made his evening smoke and headed for the rooming-house without even going up one side of the road and down the other side rattling doors, the way he usually did.

Tonight, the darned town could look after itself. It had been a sore subject with him for several years, anyway, that the chiselling Town Council of Millton neglected to hire a town-constable like all other towns did. He knew exactly why they didn't do it, too: Because they knew he would put the town to bed every night and would maintain law and order in daylight.

At the rooming-house he entered his room in the dark, lit the lamp, slowly shed his clothing and tiredly climbed into his bed. It had rope springs and a chaff-mattress but tonight it was the most luxurious thing he had ever lain out his sore and bruised and aching body upon.

FOURTEEN:
DICKSON'S PREDICTION

The wanted dodger left no doubt at all about Maxwell Dickson. Walt sat with a cup of coffee in the clear morning sunlight of the outer-office studying the thing. He had bathed and shaved, had slept like a dead man until long after sunrise, and had filled up on a breakfast steak, fried spuds and crabapplepie.

He had long ago taken a tray down to the prisoner and now he had nothing more to do until he darned well felt like doing something.

Max Dickson was wanted in Texas and

New Mexico for robbery, for felonious assault, and for abduction for ransom. The rewards totalled four hundred dollars. Max's record went back almost eleven years.

Walt put down the poster and shook his head. He was fishing out his papers and tobacco sack when the roadside door opened and a tall, black-eyed Mexican with very pale skin, walked in. The man was dressed like a *vaquero* and he looked different from just about every other Mex cowboy Walt had ever seen before.

Intuition supplied Walt with all he had to know about his visitor as he abandoned his search for the tobacco sack and arose to nod.

The Mexican had no accent at all. He gravely extended a hand and said, 'Deputy, my name is Fulgencio Delgado.'

Walt shook and gestured for Fulgencio Delgado to be seated. Instead the tall man remained standing. 'I am searching for a man by the name of Tom Dickson, Deputy, and I am sure he reached this town several days ago.'

Walt pointed to the chair again, this time with more authority. He told the Mexican his name, then he asked if his guest would care for a cup of fresh coffee, and when the tall Mexican declined, Walt said, 'Mister

Delgado . . . Tom Dickson is dead.'

The Mexican looked steadily at Walt, then finally turned and sat down.

Walt explained, and when he got down to mentioning his capture of Maxwell Dickson the tall Mexican's eyes narrowed a little. 'I would like to see this one,' he said.

Walt was agreeable. He thought he understood what the Mexican was thinking: Walt was trying to protect his prisoner, Tom Dickson. As he walked towards the cell-room door Walt said, 'Mister Delgado; put your sixgun on my desk.'

He waited. The tall Mexican did not even hesitate, he put the gun down then walked past Walt into the cell-room and Walt was sure there was a bulge under the Mexican's left arm, but he said nothing.

They stood together outside Max's cell. The prisoner had finished his breakfast and was leaning on the back-wall where a sliver of warmth came through the high little narrow, barred window. Max gazed at the tall Mexican blankly. 'Who's he?' Max asked Walt.

There was no answer for a long time, and finally Max strolled to the front bars and looked truculently out. 'What's on your mind, *Gachupin?*' he asked.

The Mexican turned slowly towards Walt.

'I didn't see him this close the only time I saw him, and it was dark. Deputy . . . ?'

Walt shook his head. 'Mister Delgado, if this was Tom I'd tell you. It isn't, it's his brother Max. Tom died when a horse threw him into a tree up in the mountains a couple of days ago.'

'You know this, Deputy?'

'Yes sir; I was there when he got hurt, only I didn't think he was hurt that badly.'

Max said, 'Hell; now I know who this is; this is the beaner who was chasing my brother!'

Walt watched Delgado, not Max Dickson. He was close enough to be positive about that shoulder-holstered gun inside Delgado's coat. But the tall Mexican turned away and walked back up to the office.

Walt followed him, closed the door as the Mexican retreived his Colt, and Walt said, 'I'm sorry. I heard from the dead one why you were after him. I don't blame you one bit.'

Delgado concentrated on settling his six-gun back into its hip-holster, with his head lowered and his face averted. 'I am sorry too,' he mumbled. 'It's been a very long trail, and I wanted it to end — differently.' He raised black eyes. 'They are the worst of the border scum, no?'

Walt could agree to that without a single reservation. He went to the desk, picked up the dodger and handed it to Delgado. As the tall Mexican read Maxwell's background his long mouth curled in cold scorn. 'Worthless,' he ground out, passing back the poster. 'Animals.'

'Worse than animals,' Walt replied, taking back the poster and tossing it back atop the desk. 'Mister Delgado . . .' He extended his hand. They shook, and the tall man finally changed expression, just a trifle. He almost smiled. Then he walked out of the jailhouse.

Walt stood a moment before returning behind his table to try again to roll a smoke. He did better this time. He had the thing rolled and lipped but unlighted when his next visitor arrived. It was Abe Dunphy who owned the general store. Abe was a very civic-minded rather stout individual, greying, with shrewd and observant brown eyes and an almost perpetual small grin down around his full-lipped mouth.

'Everyone is talking about how well you handled things,' Dunphy said, and Walt waited because he knew the storekeeper very well; Abe Dunphy never jumped right in the middle of someone, he invariably led up to it by first talking them off their guard. He was a likeable person, and although he was very opinionated, he was not the kind of a man who liked to make trouble for people. But as the Chairman of the Millton Town Council, Abe had long felt it was his responsibility to make his stand plain on matters of importance.

Now, he said, 'It would have been so much better if you'd brought in the other one, though, Walt.'

Harney's guard was down despite himself. 'Yeah, if he'd lived I'd have got him down here one way or the other, Abe.'

Dunphy's little smile lingered. 'That's my point, Walt. You should have brought back the carcass.' Dunphy's warm brown gaze softened towards the erring lawman. 'You see, if folks could have *seen* the body of the man who killed their friend, Jake Sunday . . .'

Walt stared. 'He was dead, Abe.'

'Well, did you actually see him dead, Walt?'

'No; I was two-thirds of the way back here with his brother when a — man — rode down out of there and told me Tom had died under that tree where I'd left him.'

Dunphy's smile deepened a little. 'Walt; you were dealing with the kind of men who lie and kill and steal and . . .'

'No, damn it, Abe, it wasn't one of the men from Overman who told me.'

'Who was it, then?'

Walt bit back the words and stared at Abe Dunphy. If he said, 'It was a hold-out Apache', he knew exactly what the store-keeper was going to say in return . . . 'Sure, Walt; like I already said, liars, every Indian who ever lived.'

'Who was it?' repeated Dunphy.

Walt had to answer, and he was not a liar, not even when he was cornered. 'It was an Indian,' he said, and saw the warm brown eyes change perceptibly towards him. But Dunphy did not say what was obvious, he instead walked to the stove and back, hands behind his back, then looked down at the man behind the table with an almost pity-ing expression.

'Walt; no one is going to pay a reward on that little amount of worthwhile evidence.'

'Who in hell wants a reward?' asked Walt, struggling with his temper. 'Abe; that Indian didn't lie. He had Tom Dickson's gun. You don't have an outlaw's gun unless the outlaw is dead or unconscious. In this case, dead!'

Dunphy stood lost in thought for a while then said, 'The only way to get this all above-board, Walt, would be to produce the body and haul it down here where it can be identified. Where folks can see it and be sure. Do you see that, Walt?'

Walt considered the details. Even if he could find that Apache, which was problematical, the idea of un-piling a ton or more of rocks to pull a dead man out of a crack in the mountains and tie him on a horse and bring him down to Millton aroused his adamant resistance. 'What I see,' he told the storekeeper bluntly, 'is that you have some idea you're giving me the majority local opinion, and Abe I don't think you are. In fact I think if we call a public meeting and you have your say and I have my say, folks are going to believe me — not you.' Walt arose. 'If you want to go around stirring things up, I'm going to use my authority to make up a posse to ride back into those mountains and you're going to be my number-one pick. We'll go Apache hunting as well as outlaw-hunting.'

They were like a pair of wary dogs with hackles up, with fangs faintly showing, circling stiffly.

Abe Dunphy left.

Walt was still angry ten minutes later when Ned Allen came in to say Walt's gelding needed new shoes. Walt was agreeable. 'Take him over to the forge, then,' he told the liveryman, and Ned made a careless gesture with one arm.

'Looks like a big fire 'way off back in the mountains. Looks like it's miles and miles off, over against the northwest foothills below that place where the bony pinnacle sticks up.'

Walt went outside into the roadway. There were a dozen or so other gawkers out there. Mostly, people were watching those very distant banners of lazy black smoke from the east-side plankwalk where they were equally as visible.

Abe Dunphy had got no farther than the roadway. When Walt had stood a long time studying those flames he smiled enigmatically at Abe and said, 'The Indian told the truth.' Then he returned to the jailhouse leaving Abe to figure out, if he could, what that had meant.

Walt went down to see how his prisoner was making out, but first he wrote a cryptic letter to the authorities whose names were listed along the bottom of Dickson's dodger.

He did not mention to Max that he had written that letter. It was still in his pocket, anyway, he hadn't posted it.

Max, unable to climb as high as the narrow barred slot of a window in his roadside wall, said, 'What's all the commotion about out yonder?'

'Overman is burning,' stated Walt, leaning

on the strap-steel, from out in the corridor.

Max stared. 'Burning . . . ?'

'Yeah. It's below that bony pinnacle isn't it? I think that's what you told me. Well; there's a hell of a lot of black smoke out there. Not just wood-smoke, Max; oil-smoke too. And a lot of it.'

Dickson listened to each drawled word. 'That was something everyone was awful careful about. We even had a ditch of water runnin' along in back of town just in case . . . Hell!'

Walt considered the deeply troubled look on the outlaw's face. 'I'm not especially sorry,' he murmured, and caught the glint of cold anger in the outlaw's glance as Max looked up. 'I just never liked the idea of there being a place north of the border where renegades could be safe. It was too much like putting a premium on murder and rustling and robbery . . . If you could reach Overman, like Tom tried to do, after murdering a resistin' woman — you were safe . . . I'm damned glad the place is burnt out.'

'Yeah, you would be,' exclaimed the angry prisoner. 'Your gawddamn holy-holies would be. Let me tell you something, Deputy, the only big difference between you and me and most of those fellers who were livin' up there, is that you had everything come along just right for you all the time you was growin' up, and the rest of us never got a decent lousy break in life.'

'Oh hell,' groaned Walt in disgust, and turned to walk up out of the cell-room. He did not quite reach the doorway before Max sang out after him.

'You're going to find out, Deputy. If that really is Overman burnin' out, all them fellers up there will have to leave the hills — will have to go somewhere to make a livin' . . . You'll damned well find out!'

Walt drew off a cup of tepid coffee and made a smoke to go with it. He hadn't considered the possibility that by ordering the destruction of the hornet's nest he was going to drive the hornets down around Millton.

He wasn't sure that would happen, either, as he stood and thought about it. Some of those men surely would go on over the rims and out into the northward country.

But not all of them. And furthermore, it would be easier to head southward down out of the mountains. Even so, if those men were notorious enough, they would avoid towns like Millton.

Walt drank coffee, smoked, and *hoped* they would avoid Millton, anyway.

Fifteen:
A Crisis

Two range cattlemen, weathered, tough individuals named Bronson and Haggard, were out front of the harness works when Walt went up to post a letter. As he approached those two an idea formed in his mind. After mailing the letter he went up to the cowmen and said, 'See the smoke in the mountains?'

The turkey-necked, leathery old rawboned man closest to Walt nodded. 'Yup. I understand that was the settlement them outlaws had back up there. At least that's what's being said around town.'

Walt agreed with that. 'I'm sure it was.' He eyed the cattlemen and they eyed him. One of them said, 'Deputy, is it true you fetched back a different outlaw from the feller who killed Jake Sunday?'

'I brought back the brother of the man who killed Jake.'

'Why him?'

'Well; the one who killed Jake was trying to reach his brother. I caught him first, then the horse he stole from Ned flung him into a tree and I caught the other one. Then the hurt-one died.'

'The one who shot Jake?'

'Yeah. That left me with the other one.'

'Damned complicated,' muttered one of the cowmen. 'Anyway, you got one of them . . . And we're right obliged about that.'

The pair of tough older men stared unwaveringly at Walt. For a moment the lawman wasn't sure what those looks meant, then it dawned on him, so he slowly wagged his head and said, 'Gents; you even come down to the jailhouse in the centre of the road, and I'll blow you to Kingdom Come with a shotgun. No one takes a prisoner out of my jailhouse.'

'Even if the contemptible son of a bitch deserves lynching?'

'Even then,' stated Walt, giving look for look.

'Well sir,' one of the cowmen murmured softly, pulling out a pocket-knife and opening it to carefully pare away at a fingernail, 'Deputy, between us — and some of the other outfits who been talkin' the same way since we all met at Jake's funeral — we got maybe thirty damned tough armed men.'

The cowman flicked his knife closed and raised narrowed eyes. As he pocketed the knife he straightened up as though to walk away.

Walt held them both there with harsh

words. 'You think hanging the brother of the man who killed Jake is going to make everything right again? Gents, I'll give you an idea of just how darned wrong you are. With their hideout burnt those renegades from the mountains are going to go several directions, and some of them are coming southward towards Millton and your ranges. They'll need money and horses, among other things, and they'll come skulking around like the oldtime Indians. They'll kill and steal, and you'll be piddlin' around town because you want to hang the brother of the man you'd ought to hang. You like that, gents?'

Walt perhaps should have chosen the moment he finished speaking to turn and walk southward to his jailhouse. Instead he remained up there, watching the faces of the old ranchers.

What he'd had in mind needed doing but he preferred the rangemen doing it on their own, not because he did not want to leave town and try to coordinate the patrolling of the rangeland so much as he liked the idea of the cattlemen handling something like this on their own. In their own very *final* way.

Rangelaw was different from book-law in several ways, but in its punishment it was drastically different, and Walt Harney, having been frustrated time and time again by book-law, privately preferred rangelaw. Those who said it was nothing but lynchlaw, and that it often hanged or shot the wrong man, there were those who knew a lot better.

Rangelaw was responsible for far fewer innocent victims than book-law. It was administered by men who dispensed justice with positive and cold impartiality. An eye for an eye and a tooth for a tooth.

The cowman named Haggard cocked his head a little sceptically at Walt and said, 'Deputy; you expectin' us to fetch them in to you if we catch 'em?'

Walt avoided a direct answer by saying, 'Mister Haggard, I kind of doubt that you'll be able to scoop them up like a bunch of strays. Wanted men with money on their heads don't just come along, do they?'

Old Bronson nodded. 'You don't want the carcasses, then?'

Walt was tempted to tell them to send in the bodies, if there were any, after dark, and pile them on the walk out front of Abe Dunphy's store. Instead he said, 'It's up to you; if you've got proof they fired first and got themselves killed in self-defence, and you think they might have a price on them and you want it, bring them in.'

Haggard looked pained. 'I never in my life needed that kind of money,' he grunted, and his companion nodded in dour agreement.

Walt hesitated a moment longer, then said, 'Gents . . . ?'

Bronson ignored Walt to speak to his companion. 'Jake'd favour something like this.'

Haggard agreed, then they both stepped off the plankwalk on their way over to the tie-rack where their saddle-horses patiently stood, and Walt was satisfied. Between them, Haggard and Bronson would waste no time getting the word spread over the cattle ranges that very likely renegades of the worst kind would shortly be arriving like sly wolves upon the outskirts of the cow outfits.

Walt went over to the cafe for a tray, and a bowl of chili for himself, then returned to the jailhouse cell-room and when Max bent down to pull the tray the rest of the way under the door, Walt said, 'There is lynch-talk.'

Max stood up with the tray, scowling out through the bars. 'Against me? What the hell did I do? I hardly ever came into this lousy town.'

'No one said lynch-talk has to be rational,

160

Max, all they ever said is that it sometimes starts up. The barman your brother killed was popular around Millton.'

Max took the tray to his bunk and perched over there to eat. 'Not with me he wasn't popular,' he growled, and peered. 'I get it; you went around tellin' 'em I'm the one who got my brother to shoot the bastard.'

'Nope; I didn't mention that,' stated the lawman. 'The only thing I've said so far was to the cowmen: That they'd better start patrolling their ranges and minding their horses and their homes.'

Max fell to eating. After waiting for the outlaw to speak again, and discovering that Max was not going to, Walt returned to the front office, went out front, locked the roadside door and strolled down to Ned's barn to see if his horse had been taken to the forge yet.

He had. Ned was out front sitting on a whittled old trading bench with the halter and shank lying in the dust at his feet. He looked up, then down again as he said, 'Smith'll get to him as quick as he can. He's got four animals ahead.' Then Ned looked up suddenly. 'You headin' out; you need to borrow a horse?'

Walt eased down upon the old bench. 'No. Where is Purdy?'

'Quit, by gawd. Isn't that a corker? After all the years him and me ran this place, sort of like partners, by golly he come around to my home last night, sort of late, and wanted his pay, and nothing I could say would make him change his mind.'

Walt sighed. 'He was good with livestock, Ned. Never got into any trouble and sort of minded his own business.' Walt didn't care that the dayman had undoubtedly fled the moment he saw Walt ride into town with one of the notorious renegades from Overman. The most he could have held Purdy for was abetting, and that wasn't much of a charge. Anyway, Purdy and men like Purdy had never been the people Walt Harney viewed as criminals. They were nuisances, not felons.

Ned looked at the deputy's profile. 'You feelin' better?'

Walt turned. 'What do you mean? I haven't been sick.'

'No, but you sure was disagreeable last night.'

Walt was embarrassed so he did not answer the question. Instead, he said, 'What did you do with the blood-bay?'

'Him? Oh, I sold him last night.'

Walt stared. 'Last night?'

'Well; Purdy never owned a darned horse

and it sort of rankled me that he'd up and quit me like that, without any decent notice and all.'

'So you sold him the blood-bay?'

'Yes . . . Well, what did you expect me to do with him? When a horse gets a bad reputation, Walt, you might just darned well have him on your hands until he dies of old age. I didn't want that blasted animal and Purdy hadn't heard — and anyway, I let him have the blood-bay dirt cheap. Ten dollars. He surely was worth that.'

'He wasn't worth a two cent bullet and you know it,' stated the lawman.

Old Ned spread his hands. 'It's not against the law to sell a horse. Not even one like that. Anyway, he didn't do nothing. I slipped down to the barn right after, and watched Purdy take a pad from the harness-room where the wood-stove was cracklin' and rig the horse out, mount up and ride away. So there.'

'You darned fraud. The stove was crackling and that meant the pads in the harness room were warm.'

Ned leaned back and rolled his eyes like a genuine martyr. 'Why in the hell are you pickin' on me?' he mourned. 'I'm an old boy tryin' to get by as best I can without robbin' folks or hurtin' them, and no mat-

ter what I do you come along pickin' on
me.'

Walt looked at the old man's melancholy
expression, and laughed. 'I'm not picking
on you. I came down here lookin' for the
dayman. If he's gone, well then I'll pass on
to you the same warning I passed along to
the range cowmen: Overman was burnt out.
You saw that yourself. That means those
outlaws up there have to come boilin' down
out of the mountains in search of new
horses.'

Ned sat bolt upright. This notion had
clearly not occurred to him before. 'Oh
Chriz!' he blurted out. 'I got sixteen head of
horses loose on the south range!' He sprang
up and raced down into his barn. Walt heard
him bawling for his nightman, who was
evidently doubling for the dayman until
Purdy could be replaced.

'Reg? Reg, darn you, come out of there
and saddle us a couple of horses there's
outlaws all over the south range and we got
to bring home the loose-stock! Reg, blast
you come down out'n that loft I know
you're sneakin' a snooze up there!'

Walt arose with a sigh and strode back
northward in the direction of his office. He
saw Abe Dunphy briskly hiking in the same
direction from the opposite end of town and

felt like cursing. Instead, he slowed his gait to allow the storekeeper to meet him out front, and to open the door with his big brass key and waved Dunphy in first.

Abe was upset. His customary little smile was not showing. 'I just heard that the cattlemen have knowledge that we're about to be invaded by outlaws from out of the mountains.'

Walt said nothing. It was impossible that the cowmen had that knowledge; Walt had himself only warned them a half hour earlier. But there was no denying that rumours fed upon themselves; evidently what had happened was that Bronson and Haggard had mumbled about why they were leaving town, and to whom they had mumbled had afterwards gone around embroidering the tale until here it was, coming from the storekeeper, different, vivid, and dramatic.

'Deputy, I got a wagonload of supplies on the way south through the pass. I got some bargains in supplies up at Stanhope when the mercantile up there went out of business . . . That driver and all those supplies will be about halfway through the mountains by now.'

Walt went to his table and sat down. Without a flicker of concern he said, 'What did you have in mind doing about it, Abe?'

Dunphy suddenly stiffened and glared. 'Me! What am *I* going to do about it! Walt, the town pays you to . . .'

'Whoa! Hold up just a minute,' stated the lawman. 'Abe; I'm supposed to protect the town and the surrounding area, and I'm also supposed to use my own discretion . . . Right now I figure the town is in danger, and the cow outfits, but they've got gun-handy cowboys, so that leaves your wagon-load of bargains up on the coach road somewhere. Do you know what I figure, Abe? You'd better buckle on your gun, take a rifle with you and ride up to lend your man some support. If he needs it, but I'll be damned if I can imagine why outlaws would want to stop a wagon full of traps and bolt-goods and underdrawers and door-hinges.'

Dunphy stared. 'You won't go up and escort my wagon?'

Walt shook his head. 'Nope. I've got to make a choice; your wagon or the town. I'll look out for the town. Abe . . . next time it comes to a vote with the Town Council about whether to hire a town-constable or not, take my advice and vote to hire him, because if there was one here now, I'd go up and help your man with the wagon.'

Walt sat and gave look for look with the storekeeper, until Abe Dunphy fled out into the roadway heading for the stagecoach corralyard where he thought he might possibly be able to hire a couple of rough-tough hostlers to go up the road in search of his wagon.

Sixteen: Strangers

Bruce Frisby met Walt Harney out in front of the stage office with the midday sun almost directly overhead.

As a rule, the preacher was careful of his appearance. There were few individuals in a cowtown who commanded more normal respect than ministers, and that resulted whether the people who respected them attended church regularly or not.

But this morning Bruce Frisby had been grubbing in the weed-patch out behind his rectory. Like everyone else in springtime, the preacher was readying the soil for a vegetable garden and when he met Walt Harney his hands were soiled, his powerful upper torso was encased in a sweaty old faded butternut shirt, and when Walt grinned the preacher grinned back.

'Labour for the good of your soil,' he intoned.

Walt did not pursue this beyond saying, 'Does that mean you got to get down on your knees in the dirt, Bruce? Well, anyway, I'm beginning to feel normal again.'

Preacher Frisby's smile faded. 'I wouldn't become too settled and comfortable, Deputy. They tell me Millton is going to be raided by outlaws within the next forty-eight hours.'

Walt looked sardonic. 'Abe tell you that?'

'No, but his clerk did.'

'That's what I figured Bruce, I doubt that we'll be raided. At least if a screen of armed rangeriders flung out all across the range to the north, east and west can prevent it, we won't be. I sort of stirred up the cowmen this morning with that same sort of story, only I had their remudas being rustled.'

Frisby ran a soiled big hand down across his jaw and peered up the roadway where a stagecoach was rattling down to a slow approach at the outskirts of town. 'Had a nice talk with a *vaquero* named Delgado last evening,' he said, never taking his eyes off the six-horse hitch and stage. 'He needed assurance.'

'About what? That I hadn't lied to him?'

'Yes.' Frisby looked back at the lawman. 'I

gave him the assurance. I saw him ride out of town heading southeastward very early this morning.' Bruce shook his head. 'Even when you've got faith it's hard to keep from questioning the wisdom of things that happen, sometimes.'

Walt nodded. 'That's what keeps sinners like me and a hell of a lot of other fellers from being able to knuckle under.'

Frisby shrugged mighty shoulders. He had not liked that term 'knuckle under' but he made no issue of it. 'In time,' he said, and turned back to watch the stagecoach halt out front of the corralyard while three men alighted. He studied them for a while then said, 'Walt, look behind you; I've never been able to tell from their looks whether they are outlaws or lawmen. Why is that? Because they all have that same uncompromising expression of menace?'

Walt turned without answering Preacher Frisby. The three men who had alighted from the southbound stage were indeed lanky and unsmiling and armed with the tied-down weapons of one breed or the other. It hadn't occured to Walt before, but it did now as he stood across the road looking.

Those could be three U.S. marshals, at least *deputy* U.S. marshals, or they could in fact be escapees from the fire back at Over-man, although if that were the case they would have had to have made excellent haste in leaving the gutted settlement and reaching the north-south coach-road in time to flag down the southbound stage and arrive in Millton this soon.

He said, 'Mind all that dirt under your fingernails,' and left the minister standing over there watching as Walt struck out on a diagonal course towards the stage-station.

As soon as he had shed his passengers the driver talked up his hitch, cut a very wide sashay, and came around out of the wide roadway arrow-straight into the corralyard past the log gate-post without so much as dusting a hub.

Others hadn't been that skilled. Those posts had scars on top of scars from former hubs and wheels.

Two of the tall strangers were standing slightly apart from the third man, gazing disconsolately at the closed saloon. When Walt approached the third man, who had grey at the temples which made him look very distinctive, this stranger dropped an unsmiling steady look upon the badge, then upon the man wearing it, and raised a big hand to run the back of it along beneath his

droopy moustache as he said, ''Evenin',
Deputy.'

It was barely midday. Walt nodded. 'Welcome to Millton. The saloon is out of business, otherwise there is a card-room and a
pool-hall.'

The big unsmiling man said, 'Rooming-
house?'

Walt pointed. 'Yonder on this same side of
the road. I live up there so I can recom-
mend the place. The beds beat sleeping on
the ground and they always give you two
glasses of lemonade before supper so's you
won't eat very much. Otherwise I'd recom-
mend the cafe across from the jailhouse.'

The tall man's hard, penetrating eyes
almost showed warmth, and if there were
ever a smile lurking beneath the thick,
droopy moustache, it would be impossible
to see unless the lanky older man actually
smiled, which at the present time he avoided
having to do by reaching slowly into a coat
pocket and just as slowly bringing forth the
left hand with the dull little circlet on his
palm. Inside the steel circlet was the small
slightly concave star and the encircling
words, 'Deputy United States Marshal.'
Below that were two more words. 'Denver
Colorado.'

'Bates,' said the tall man, and did not

deign to introduce his dolorous companions who were still regarding the closed saloon as though such a thing were just about unimaginable, and as a matter of fact it was.

'Come down from Raton,' said the deputy federal marshal. 'There is a settlement hereabouts, deputy, that harbours outlaws. We got orders to clean it up or blow it down. You got any idea about where it's at?'

Walt judged the deputy marshal and decided he had known a lot of men just like him. 'It burned down,' he told Bates. 'In fact I think you'll still be able to see the smoke if you ride up-country to the foothills.'

Bates looked stonily at Walt. 'When did it burn down?' he asked with obvious scepticism.

'I guess it got fired up some time yesterday, but the smoke was visible this morning.'

'You got any idea who'd burn it out, Deputy?'

Walt smiled. 'If you're going to ride up there, Marshal,' he said, 'you'll run into outlaws riding out, down this way maybe, since now they've all got to find a new place to roost. Maybe some of them would tell you what happened. I've been down here since the place caught fire.'

'You ever been up to that place?' asked

Marshal Bates, and Walt was still smiling when he shook his head. 'No, but I have a prisoner in my jailhouse who used to live up there. You're welcome to talk to him if you care to . . . I started up there a few days back, and ran into a few little set-backs which fixed things so I didn't have to go all the way.'

The unsmiling, ponderously large and important man stroked his moustache again, looking at Walt as though he, too, had arrived at a private judgment about another cowtown deputy.

'Sometimes it don't take much,' he murmured.

Walt's smile slipped a notch. 'Mind explaining what you meant by that?' he asked, but the large man was grumbling for his two companions to come along and either did not hear or chose to ignore Walt's remark. When he faced around again he was gazing along the roadway.

'Where's the liverybarn?' he asked.

Walt pointed. 'Lower end of town. You want to talk to that prisoner of mine?'

Marshal Bates was scornful. 'Naw; anyone you caught, son, won't be the kind of fish we're used to anglin' for. Come along, fellers,' he said to his companions and the three of them started southward.

Walt watched them go. It occurred to him that Fate could have been kinder to him by allowing old Ned still to have that blood-bay down at the barn to lease out.

Abe Dunphy walked over from his store balling up the apron he'd just removed as he came along. He was gazing after those three federal officers.

'Walt,' he called briskly. 'Who are those gents?'

'Federal deputies,' replied the deputy, and decided Fate had not completely deserted him. 'And if you hurry, Abe, maybe you can catch up before they get horses from Ned and head out for the mountains.'

Dunphy came to life. 'The mountains? Northward, by any chance?'

'Yup, they're goin' outlaw-hunting up at Overman. But if they stuck to the roadway they might find your wagon and . . .'

Abe spurted off down the roadway clutching his balled-up apron. He did not catch the tall men until they had already disappeared from Walt's view into the liverybarn, but Abe ran on until he also disappeared down there.

Walt walked to the wall-bench in front of the jailhouse, sat down, thumbed back his hat, rolled a smoke and had it lighted before

Abe re-appeared walking back up the plank-walk.

Walt stretched his legs, got comfortable, and waited. When the storekeeper came up he halted and looked almost mournfully downward. 'I'm going to write the Territorial Representative in Congress. Walt, that marshal was the most scornful, humiliatin', insulting and disagreeable lawman I've ever run across.'

'Disagreeable about what?' Walt asked innocently.

'They are manhunters, he told me. They are professional outlaw-exterminators and people like me had a hell of a nerve insulting them by asking if they'd go hunt up a wagonload of store-goods and escort it. He said people like me had better learn respect.'

'What did you say, Abe?'

Dunphy reddened. 'When you were talking to him, did he open his coat? Well; he did when I was there. Ned and I both saw it; he is wearing a sixshooter tied low and with the butt reversed for one of those border-cross draws . . . That gunstock had seven notches cut in it, Walt . . . What did I say? Not a blessed word. What would *you* have said?'

Walt considered ash on his smoke as he also said, 'Not a blessed word.' Then he

175

smiled upwards. 'Couldn't hire any corral-yard bums to ride up there either?'

'How did you know I tried?'

'I didn't know it, Abe, I just know you. Couldn't hire any?'

'No one wants to ride into the mountains what with all the stories going around about outlaws fanning out all up through there like rabid wolves. No; I couldn't hire anyone.'

Up the roadway northward a man sang out and both the idlers in front of the jailhouse craned around. Remotely visible up the coach-road several miles was a slow-moving faded green wagon being pulled by four big stout mules.

Abe Dunphy looked, and gasped. 'My gawd, it's my rig. Look up there, Walt. It's my rig and he got through all those lousy outlaws!'

Abe went loping up the road northward as swiftly as he'd previously gone loping after the federal officers southward, and this time Walt also idly watched.

Southward, three riders emerged from Ned's barn and also turned northward up the main roadway. Walt watched them too. When they got abreast of his jailhouse not a one of them looked. Bates was sitting erect and with overwhelming importance. As he treated the townsmen to the sight of a genuine U.S. deputy marshal on a manhunt, he lifted his left hand in that way he had, and with a flourish ran it beneath his droopy moustache.

Walt flicked his cigarette into the roadway, sighed and shook his head, then he arose to go over to the cafe.

Seventeen: 'Hell!'

Shortly after Dunphy's wagon reached town a cowboy named Cotton Redford who worked for Old Man Haggard arrived at the cafe looking for the deputy sheriff.

Haggard's men had spied a small band of riders emerging cautiously from the northward mountains driving a band of loose-stock ahead of them. Haggard had waited until the strangers were fully in the open then he had led his riders in a howling attack which had scattered the strangers like quail.

Now, Haggard had fifteen head of someone's horses in a corral at the ranch and wanted the deputy in Millton to send back word whether or not he should bring the horses to town to be impounded in the local public corrals.

Walt said, 'Don't recognize any of their brands?'

The cowboy shook his head. 'The old man even looked it up in the brand book. Sure as hell ain't marks none of us ever saw before.'

'Yeah, might as well bring them along. We'll advertise and impound,' said Walt, and gazed at the sun-tanned youthful rider. 'Ever get close to the men who had been driving them?'

'Nope. We sure-Lord tried, but them boys busted out like the devil and his imps was behind 'em. Sure as hell they was renegades . . . Mister Haggard says next time by gawd we're goin' to go shooting.'

Walt was considering a mild admonition about that when the cowboy spoke again.

'The Bronson and Crawford crews are also riding the foothills. I'll tell you for a plumb fact, Deputy, if an outlaw gets through us he'll have to be invisible or have wings . . . There was three fellers headin' north that Bronson and his crew went after.'

Walt stared. 'Catch 'em?'

'Nope; them boys also taken off like they'd been fired out of cannon. Old Bronson went after 'em in his usual no-nonsense manner.'

Walt winced. '. . . Not shooting?'

'Yeah; hell we could hear the gunfire five miles off. They run them three strangers up into the mountains and the last Bronson and his boys seen, them three fellers was riding with their coat-tails standing straight out behind.'

Walt arose, dropped enough silver to cover what he had eaten and walked outside with Cotton Redford. It would not do one bit of good, now, to explain that those three strangers wearing those clawhammer coats had been deputy U.S. marshals.

Walt gazed at the sun. It was still high. He guessed Marshal Bates and his cohorts would not try to reach Millton now, until late night when they could skulk their way back.

Cotton said, 'I'll tell the old man, and we'll haze in them horses.' He stirred dust with a scuffed boot-toe, then also said, 'You know, Deputy, them boys from Overman aren't goin' to feel welcome down here, and they're goin' to pass along the word about that. Too bad; chasin' fellers like that sure beats hell out of trailin' up someone's darned old gummer cows.'

Walt nodded. He had heard that said elsewhere, and not too long before, but right now he could not recall the circumstances. He said, 'I'll tell Ned to leave the corral gates open . . . One more thing: You tell Mr Haggard if he sees Mr Bronson, to hail anyone they see on the range, first, before they start shooting.'

Redford bobbed his head. 'Sure,' he agreed, and went to his horse whistling. By the time he got back to the ranch he would not remember to pass along that admonition and Walt knew it.

Well, Marshal Bates picked an awfully poor time to go riding out towards the mountains, because if he hadn't run into a lot of excited cowmen, farther along he would probably have run into a lot of equally disturbed renegades, and the difference was that cowmen would give chase and whoop it up, and fire their guns and primarily succeed in scaring hell out of those rented horses the lawmen were riding — but the outlaws would bushwhack the lawmen and kill them, and that was a hell of a lot different.

Also, Walt made a fresh pot of coffee in his office so that when the furious U.S. lawmen came stealthily back to town he could give them something while they were profanely denouncing the cowmen of the Millton territory, probably Millton as well, its deputy and its citizenry.

He didn't blame them. Being fired at and

chased by a band of wild rangemen was a hair-raising experience, and granting that rangemen were the worst gunshots in the world, even a posse of blind folks, if they threw enough lead, had to score an occasional hit.

Later, Walt took a supper tray down to his prisoner. Max accepted it beneath the door and set it aside as he eyed the lawman. 'I figured a way to increase that two thousand dollars I got cached away to four thousand,' he told Walt. 'Deputy; you got any idea how long a man could live like a lord on four thousand dollars?'

Walt had an idea. 'Long enough to ruin his liver and his chingalee.'

'You interested? Just open that door and look the other way.'

'I wouldn't be interested if I lived to a thousand and each year you increased it another couple of thousand, Max. You like that answer?'

'You're a bastard, Deputy, did you know that!'

'No I didn't, and I don't think it's right, either.' Walt stood gazing through the bars. 'You play checkers, Max?'

'Everybody plays checkers,' growled the disgruntled outlaw.

'Good. Because I got a feeling that before

those lawmen from Texas and New Mexico come after you, we're going to have set around here many a night playing checkers.'

'Bastard,' ground out the renegade as Walt turned to go back to his office.

Abe Dunphy arrived within moments of the time when Walt dampened the stove under his grimy old coffeepot. Walt smiled at the storekeeper. He was not especially fond of Dunphy but Walt smiled easily, which concealed a lot about him people usually never even suspected. For example, seeing that smile now, the storekeeper dropped into a chair and said, 'I guess I got carried away, wanting to see that outlaw's carcass . . . I mean the one who shot Jake.'

'I know who you meant,' stated Walt, holding up the pot. 'Care for some coffee?'

'No thanks,' said the storekeeper, whose glance at the dented, unwashed old pot showed frank revulsion, and that was another thing which set them apart; Walt Harney was a bachelor and saw nothing particularly objectionable about a coffeepot which hadn't been scrubbed out in a month, while the storekeeper was a married man who was accustomed to clean and sparkling coffeepots.

Walt half-filled a cup, tasted the coffee, then strolled to his table to sit behind it. It wasn't *good* coffee, but neither was it *bad* coffee. Well; not terrible coffee anyway.

'Good thing you changed your mind about seeing the body of Tom Dickson,' he told the storekeeper, 'because I never had the faintest notion of going up there and trying to find it for you.'

'He's dead all right,' stated Abe. 'My driver met a couple of young buckaroos heading over the pass northward. They didn't come right out an tell him they were from Overman but he guessed it. One of them said they'd seen the settlement burn to the ground from a sidehill behind and above. They also said it was In'ians burnt the place out, and one of those redskins rode up the slope and told them to get out while they were able or he'd kill them like the man he'd buried whose pistol he was holding. The pistol had the initials T.D. cut into the stock. Tom Dickson; do you see?'

Walt 'saw'. 'This isn't bad coffee, Abe,' he said, 'I've got plenty.'

'No thanks. I really have got to get home for supper.' Dunphy arose. 'Something else those men told my driver: Most of the men from Overman didn't want to come down here. They'd heard the law around Millton was mean and bad.' Abe stepped to the door. 'That'd be you.'

Walt said, 'Yeah,' and held up his coffee cup.

Dunphy departed.

Walt slowly lowered the cup, gazed at its black, oily contents, then with a slight shudder put it aside. The little things which were important to a man hadn't been going quite right for Walt lately. Ned had got rid of the blood-bay before that egotistical deputy U.S. marshal arrived in town, and just now he hadn't been able to get any of this fresh batch of corrosive coffee down Abe Dunphy.

He went to the cell-room door and called. 'Hey, Max; you want a cup of fresh coffee?'

A moment later the reply came echoing up from the dingy vault. 'Who made it?'

'Well, you darnfool, who do you figure made it?'

'Yas, that's what I thought,' boomed the caged outlaw. 'No, I don't want none of it. You know what you'd ought to do with it? Give it to that liveryman who lets people get hold of mankillin' horses and thinks that's funny!'

Walt closed the door, barred it, went out front and rolled a cigarette in the late-day shadows. It was over; all of it was over with, except for some upstart lawmen sneaking back into town tonight, and the way he felt about that at this moment, for everything unpleasant they would say to *him,* he had something just as unpleasant to say to *them.*

He lit the smoke, savoured the bite and aroma of it, watched the stranger over in front of Jake's saloon throw open the doors from the inside, and decided since the stranger resembled Jake so much, it had to be his legitimate heir.

And that would signify the true end of all the hectic unpleasantness; if Jake's place was open for business again exactly as it had been the day before Walt Harney had ridden off looking for Sunday's killer — a week earlier, last Sunday, in fact — then regardless of the death, the burn-out, the weariness, hunger, fear, desperation and near-death which had transpired since, maybe everything had happened for the best after all.

'Hell,' he said aloud, flipping away the smoke as he stepped off the plankwalk into the dust heading for the saloon. 'Don't any of it ever make a hell of a lot of sense.'

We hope you have enjoyed this Large Print book. Other Thorndike, Wheeler, and Chivers Press Large Print books are available at your library or directly from the publishers.

For information about current and upcoming titles, please call or write, without obligation, to:

Publisher
Thorndike Press
295 Kennedy Memorial Drive
Waterville, ME 04901
Tel. (800) 223-1244

or visit our Web site at:

www.gale.com/thorndike
www.gale.com/wheeler

OR

Chivers Large Print
published by BBC Audiobooks Ltd
St James House, The Square
Lower Bristol Road
Bath BA2 3SB
England
Tel. +44(0) 800 136919
email: bbcaudiobooks@bbc.co.uk
www.bbcaudiobooks.co.uk

All our Large Print titles are designed for easy reading, and all our books are made to last.